My Life at First Try

MY LIFE

AT

FIRST TRY

a novel

Mark Budman

COUNTERPOINT BERKELEY

The author and publisher gratefully acknowledge the editors
who have previously published chapters from this novel:
"Country Roads" in *Gowanus*; an excerpt from "Two and One
Nights" in *Weird Tales*; "To Own the Block" and "A Patriotic Angel"
in *Mississippi Review*; an excerpt from "Cat's Magic" in *Binnacle*;
"Keep Sawing, Shura" in *Stone Canoe*; "Down Came the Rain" in
Gator Springs Gazette; "Twelve Steps Down" in *SmokeLong Quarterly*.

Library of Congress Cataloging-in-Publication Data
Budman, Mark.
My life at first try : a novel / Mark Budman.
p. cm.
ISBN-13: 978-1-58243-400-1
ISBN-10: 1-58243-400-X
1. Jews, Russian—Fiction. 2. Siberia (Russia)—Fiction.
3. Emigration and immigration—Fiction. 4. Russians—
United States—Fiction. 5. Immigrants—Fiction. 6. New York
(State)—Fiction. 7. Suburban life—Fiction. I. Title.
PS3602.U335M92 2008   813'.6—DC22
2008013092

Cover design by Jeff Clark
Interior design by David Bullen

Printed in the United States of America

COUNTERPOINT
2117 Fourth Street
Suite D
Berkeley, CA 94710
www.counterpointpress.com

Distributed by Publishers Group West

10   9   8   7   6   5   4   3   2   1

To my daughter Elizabeth, my first critic and editor.

I will love you always.

Contents

My Life at First Try

The First Song

It's 1954. I am four. My mother in her black fur coat and *valenkies*, felt boots, pulls me in a sled over the crisp Siberian snow. Fur is still cheap at this latitude. My two-year-old brother sits behind me. His mittened hands are clutching my sleeves.

I am a reindeer driver. I sing a song about what I see. I sing about a tractor pulling a wooden pole behind it to clear the road of snow. I sing about the general store where a giant poster the color of squished strawberries shows a worker and peasant hammering enemies of the state. I sing about a man lying on the sidewalk with his face down. He's probably drunk, but I sing that the enemies shot him for defending the village. I sing about two men hitting each other in the face. They must be boxers in training, ready to defend my country. I sing about a policeman in his squirrel hat, its earflaps down, in his greatcoat made of deerskin, criss-crossed by shiny leather belts. A rifle is slung over his back. He says, "Move along, folks, move along," to the people who watch the boxers. He is one great-looking warrior. If I were in charge, I would give him a medal. I sing about a girl in another sled, who lifts the scarf from the bottom of her face momentarily to stick her tongue out at me. I think it's a girl because she wears a red coat while my brother's and mine are black. I also have a scarf over my mouth. My words come out garbled, as if I am a foreigner, which I am not yet.

When I learn the alphabet, I'll write this song down.

We live in a wooden house. One room is for my family, and the second is for the Petrovs. There is a rug that hangs from the wall, above my pillow, with rabbits, squirrels and hedgehogs. I wish them goodnight before I fall asleep. On the other wall, there is a poster of a grinning soldier playing an accordion. His teeth are white, as if he's a kid.

Comrade Petrov is a butcher. That's what my grandmother says. But butchers cut meat. The Petrovs eat only potatoes, lentil soup, bread and garlic. Their son Mishka is my age.

"What's your name?" he said when we first met.

"Sasha."

"That's a girl's name."

"No. It's Alexander. Like the great king."

"What the hell is king?"

"King is a foreign tsar."

"You're named after a tsar?"

Mishka told me that his dad killed five men in a fight. He can bend a horseshoe with his fingers, carries a big knife, and he has tattoos all over. Mishka also told me that his sister Masha couldn't piss on the wall. I pity her. Even my two-year-old brother can do that, and Masha is already ten.

In the evenings, my mother reads us Longfellow in Bunin's translation while we all drink tea imported from India. I don't know what India is, except that everyone calls it our friend. I like Hiawatha. He could pass for a Russian.

I ask my father how many people he killed. He says that he shot at the Germans during the war, but he doesn't know if he got any.

Last summer, two prisoners, released after Stalin's death, tried to grab me while I was playing in my backyard. My grandma saved me. She just took an ax, and they ran away. She is so strong. She has no rifle, but she can split a log with one blow. Her name is Annie. It's the nicest girl name in the world.

My grandpa is even stronger. He could grab a bear by its paw, spin it over his head, and throw it all the way to the taiga's edge. My father is a teacher. He knows everything.

Stalin sent my grandparents here to chop wood, and my parents volunteered to live with them. That's how we got here. I don't know this yet, and I already forgot about the two prisoners. Mishka doesn't like Stalin either. He says that he's a mothersucker. When I asked what it means, Mishka said that it's a grown-up who still sucks his mother's titties.

When I see Stalin's portraits, I whisper, *mothersucker*. He's got a big mustachio, so he probably tickles his mother's tits. I've never seen her portraits, but she deserves it because she raised a son like that. She probably has tits like the witches in Macbeth. My mother says it's too early for me to read the book, but I saw the pictures already. Now, my breath settles on my scarf and turns to ice as fast as I exhale. My song streams wide and fast, like a Siberian river in the summer. I am a happy reindeer driver.

Grammar

It's 1957. I am seven. *We are not slaves. Slaves are not us.* Even in Russian, a language with a more forgiving grammar than English, that second sentence is barely grammatical. Yet Idea Vasil'evna, our first grade teacher, forces us to write it in our notebooks. She has no choice. It's printed in our textbooks. What's written by a pen can't be struck out by an ax.

We dip our pens into the inkwells, stick our tongues out and write, "*р-а-б-ы . . .*" I hate how the ink smells—like scarlet fever. The pigtails of the girl in front of me beg to be pulled but I restrain myself. I'm a man.

We know that we live in a Socialist society, but we are ready for the next step in the path of progress. That's what Idea Vasil'evna said before the class began. She is wise and motherly.

She drums the beat on her desk with a ruler. Occasionally, she goose-steps the aisles, and cranes her neck to check our progress. When she does that, our hands shake. She hits the boys on the fingers with the ruler and returns to her desk. She never hits the girls. Their fingers are delicate, like ivory netsuke, and their tears shoot out too easily. She smells like the perfume store, only stronger.

Above the teacher's desk, sweet Grandfather Lenin observes us with glee. If he could, he would jump out from his gilded frame, take away Idea Vasil'evna's ruler, and drum our fingers with it. He would never spare the girls.

His portrait is off-center, and next to it, there is a painted-over spot. Kids say that it had Stalin's portrait hanging there once. A few years before, these leaders would have jumped out together, and divided the responsibilities. Joseph, you go to the right, and I will take the left. Don't spare the rod, Joseph.

Joseph would nod, grinning under his sardonic mustache. Afterwards, back in his frame, he would light a pipe. Lenin would squint like a tomcat with the belly full of mice.

But now, Lenin is lonely.

The bell rings. We run into the school yard, which is surrounded by a heavy iron fence. We scream. We jump up and down. We chase each other. Two older boys, maybe even sixth graders, get into a fistfight, and we watch. One boy falls and the other kicks him in the ribs. The school principal comes out and positions himself by the gates. He looks like a statue in the town square, but without a horse. Iron face. Endless shoulders. A raised hand. His clothes are the color of dust. Does he have shiny, polished balls like the horse in the square? He coughs into a bullhorn. Everyone quiets, even the boy on the ground. The principal speaks.

I can make out only some words. Party. Lenin. Happy childhood. American imperialism. Five-year plan. When I grow up, I will draw posters and write big words with a red pen.

Yesterday, I saw a group of foreign tourists in downtown. They stood so straight and laughed loudly like kids, as if no one was watching them. They were dressed in shiny, neat clothing and their voices sounded like the cry of the birds heading west. I want to be a foreigner.

The bell rings again.

We return to the next class. A banner hangs along the length of the aisle. *The Party solemnly proclaims: this generation of the Soviet people will live in a Communist society.* That's progress. One plus one is two. Slaves are not us, and will never be.

Annie?

IT'S STILL 1957. I am still seven. Father unfolds a letter from Uncle Michael once again and reads it to my brother and me. At first, he reads it in English, and when he sees that we don't understand, he sighs and translates it into Russian. This is the second letter in as many years, though Father hasn't replied to the first one. He says that it's too dangerous to correspond with a foreigner, let alone a Westerner.

From this letter, we learn that Uncle Michael wants to go to college to get an engineering degree and that he has a child, a daughter named Annie.

Volodya and I scowl. A girl, phew!

Uncle also inquires if Father ever went to college. When he gets to this point, we laugh. Father teaches at a college, so there! Father stops us.

Uncle Michael sends his photograph. He has big ears, hair that sticks out all over, and a wide grin. We never smile for the camera. Father says that photography is an important and expensive business.

We already know, from the previous letter, that Uncle Michael, father's cousin, lives in Pittsburgh. Father forced us to memorize the city's spelling.

Father says that Uncle Michael is ten years younger than him and that he left the Soviet Union with his family as a child. He was called Misha then. After Father's done reading, he lets us admire the stamp. It has the American flag on it. I like it more than a simple Soviet one, but my brother says that it's too busy.

"Too busy?" Where did a five-year-old learn words like that?

I go to my grandparents' room to tell them the news about Annie.

When I enter, my grandparents stop talking and turn to me. It's a small, dark room with a bed and a tiny table. On the wall there is a lithograph of three Russian knights side by side, with their swords half-drawn.

My grandparents used to speak Yiddish to each other so I wouldn't understand them, but that didn't last long. I never learned to speak it, but I soon understood it. As my mother said, I have a talent for languages. That makes me proud. Because I'm talented, because they know it, and because Volodya is not talented.

It's funny about the languages. Everyone around here knows a few. My father says that we are like Switzerland, only without chocolate.

Russian is my main language, of course. I think in Russian and when I fight with Volodya or other kids, we cuss each other in Russian. Russian is the language of books, newspapers, school and radio. The cops, the bus drivers and the store clerks speak in Russian. Ukrainian is almost like Russian, but it sounds funny like the speaker is drunk. The Ukrainian kids say the same thing about Russian. The Moldovan language is also for school, but we study it only once a week. Kids say that Moldovan is the language of peasants. I also thought so until Father read us Eminescu. English, which we also learn once a week, sounds military, like someone is barking commands. Yiddish sounds like someone is constantly making jokes or cursing. Sometimes it's both.

"Grandma, grandma, there is an American girl, and her name is also Annie!" I shout. "Is it wicked or what?"

"That's nice," Grandma says. "It's good that you told me. But don't tell that to the other kids."

"And 'wicked' is a bad word," Grandpa says. "What's wrong with 'wonderful'?"

I sit on the couch between them and they embrace me from both sides. Of course, nothing is wrong with 'wonderful,' but it's not 'wicked.' 'Wonderful' is an adult word. I say words like that in my Russian class to impress the teacher.

"You guys moved a lot," I say. "Do you like to move?"

"Your Grandma hates moving," Grandpa says. "She's like a cat, but a bit taller and she never catches mice. Cats are always attached to the house."

"There is nothing wrong with cats," Grandma says. "The first time I moved was when I married your Grandpa. I was twenty then. The second time was when the War started. I was forty. Your Grandpa hates to move also. He's like an oak tree, but a bit smarter. Oak trees have long roots."

"There is nothing wrong with oaks," Grandpa says.

When I become a foreigner, I'll visit my uncle and tell him that I can spell Pittsburgh. I will also check out this Annie girl. Is she as yucky as the Russian girls? I hope she's like my Grandma, only younger, because I don't like wrinkles. I want to know. When I really want something, I always get it.

I don't tell this to my grandparents. I don't want to scare anyone. I sit warm and safe, like the middle knight on the lithograph. Even Stalin wouldn't dare come here. I just enjoy sitting between my grandparents, while I can.

Gander

It's 1958. I am eight. We have moved to the Kazakh city of Semipalatinsk. Comrade Stalin is long dead but not buried. He sleeps next to Grandfather Lenin in the mouse'o'leum. My father promises to take me there when we go to Moscow.

I walk home from school on the street lined with wooden fences. They are so tall that I can't see the houses except for their tin roofs. It's still chilly, and I wear a rubber coat, loose cotton pants called *sharovary* and rubber boots. I hold a thin stick in my hand because it's a sword, and I'm a knight.

In the house that has a white fence, red gate and two still-naked apple trees, lives a gander. The gate is always open and he wanders outside to bite me. He shouts *ga-ga-ga* and flip-flops his wings, big like a dragon's. I am afraid of him. In school today, they taught us that the capital of Kazakhstan is Almaty, which means "Father of Apples" in the Kazakh language, but the sight of the gander flushes from my head this useless knowledge.

I try to straighten up to look taller. My backpack holds me down. I raise my sword but the gander is not afraid. Last time I ran away.

"*Kolbit*," I shout at the gander. "*Kolbit!*" That's what the Russian kids call the Kazakh kids at school.

An ancient Kazakh woman comes out, takes my sword, and hits the gander with it. He runs.

"*Kolbit* is a bad word," she says to me, returning my weapon. She speaks Russian funny. She smells like wet chicken. When she turns away, I shake my sword at her.

At home, I tell my mother, "A *kolbit* gander attacked me. He was big. I hit him with a stick and he ran away."

She slaps me. "*Kolbit* is a bad word. Would you like if someone calls you kike?"

The other day she explained to me that we are Jewish.

"It's a nationality," she said. "Karl Marx was a Jew. Yakov Sverdlov, the first president of the Russian Soviet Republic, was a Jew."

"Can animals have nationality?" I ask. "Is Froggy Jewish?"

Froggy is my grandfather's horse. She pulls his milk delivery carriage. She's not green, but she likes sugar. I rode in the carriage several times, and all the boys were jealous, and all the girls stuck out their tongues at me.

"No. Only humans can be Jewish."

Now, I drop off my backpack and run outside. In the back of the yard, I find my brother cutting something into the bark of an apple tree with a penknife. He sees me coming but doesn't stop.

"I killed a gander today," I say, squatting next to him. He is cutting a backward K.

"What's a gander?" he asks.

"It's a dragon. I killed him with a sword. You saw my sword, right?"

He wipes the snot from his nose with the sleeve of his rubber coat. "Did he breathe fire?"

"No. It's a Kazakh dragon. Only Russian dragons breathe fire."

He nods. The next letter is O. It's an easy letter. Even five-year-olds can do it. But even if he fails, his older brother will help him.

The Monster

It's 1959. I am nine. I'm hunting for my first tiger. I crawl through the bush with my twenty-bore rifle on my shoulder. My seven-year-old brother follows me, carrying my ammunition. I spot some movement in the grass. I raise my rifle, aim, and squeeze the trigger. I hear a loud yelp like a hundred cats being hit by a thousand stones.

I cut my way with my machete through the undergrowth and come to the body. Here he is, the king of the jungle. I turn to my brother who always cheers my skill with the rifle. Now, he stands with his eyes round and his mouth opened as if he sees a monster with claws and fangs.

"It's a kitten," my brother mouths.

"Oh, foolish slave," I say. "Your eyes are clouded with fear. Look at me! I'm a hunter. I'm your *sahib*. It's a tiger. Remember how mommy read us Kipling? How the hunter uncased a twelve-bore rifle? That's what I did. Uncased a rifle and shot the beast."

Of course he remembers. He asked what twelve-bore means. Twice. I also wanted to know, but let him ask all the questions so he wouldn't think I don't have the answers.

"It's a small kitten," my brother says. He begins to cry.

"You're a girl," I say. I step forward to slap him. I'm a hero, and he's a pussy. A hero has to kick a pussy's ass or he's not a hero anymore. And if he's not a hero, someone else will kick *his* ass.

I wait for him to say, "I'll tell on you," but he doesn't.

A few days ago, our neighbor, an adult, died. The kids on the street said that he died because he scalded his birthmark. I kept peaking through my bedroom windows hoping to see his body, but I couldn't.

Then I saw four fully grown men carrying his casket. He was probably heavy. In Kipling's stories, tigers were big and heavy, too.

So I look at the slain beast again. My brother is right. My rifle is really a slingshot, and my brother carries just a bag of round stones. My machete is a pair of garden scissors. The beast is not a tiger. It's a dead kitten. It has a white belly and white socks on its front paws.

I drop my slingshot and scissors and run. I turn around the house, climb over the fence, and speed down to the pond. I'm crying like I'm a five-year-old pussy. Something is pricking my bare calves, but I feel no pain. I take off my shoes, wet the soles in the water, and scrape them against each other. My heart beats as fast as probably the kitten's heart did five minutes ago.

I like this place. I come here to launch a rubber motorboat while my brother is watching. I call the boat Santa Maria. I'm Columbus, and my brother is an Indian slave. After playing with the boat, I listen to the hordes of frogs croaking, and wish my parents bought me a rifle. If not a twelve-bore then at least a daisy gun. I call my brother Pocahontas because he's not listening to me, and because he's a girl.

Now, the pond is different. The sun beats my face like a school-yard bully. I see everything sharp and focused like through a magnifying glass. A dragonfly lands on the top of a bush next to me. A grasshopper leaps onto my knee and then hops away. An ant climbs up a dandelion's stem, and I watch it as if I have never seen its kind before. A black, armored fly is buzzing overhead.

My hands feel sticky though there is no blood on them. I kneel to wash my hands in the water. I scream. I see a monster with claws and fangs in the calm surface of the pond. He's hunting me, and there is nothing I can do to protect myself, no matter how cute I am or how sweetly I can purr.

I'll break my slingshot in a thousand pieces if I get out of here alive, and will drown them in the Ganges River.

The Tale

It's 1961. I am eleven. My brother and I lie on a folding bed, facing one another like two knaves on a playing card, and tickle each other's feet. We call the process of tickling *badya-bochki*, a made-up word. Our parents can't afford more than one bed, but the state of our family finances doesn't bother us. When tired of *badya-bochki*, I tell my brother a tale. This tale has been going on for a long time. Unlike most modern stories, it's interactive. Not a round robin, but we participate at the same time. I'm the author and the protagonist, and my brother is the main character.

When we first started the tale, last year, I said, "The protagonist is the main character. There is only one main thing of everything, boy. What do they teach you in second grade?"

"Not fair," he said. "You are the author and the main character. Who am I? Your slave? We don't have slaves in the Soviet Union."

"Don't you talk back to me. You have to be the secondary."

"Bupkis. I'm also the main or I'm leaving."

He had no place to go, of course. It was 9 PM, it was snowing outside, and he wore nothing but my old pajamas.

"That's against the rules," I said.

"But you said that the author makes up the rules."

What could I say? He got me. I agreed. I'm still the author, of course.

Now, I am telling the tale. I practically whisper in his ear, so our parents won't hear me and force us to sleep. We are Great Patriotic War officers, and we are parachuted behind the German lines. We are tall and handsome. We are very muscular. We have guns, grenades and steel helmets. Our chests are criss-crossed by bullet belts. I'm a captain and my brother is a lieutenant (OK, OK, senior lieutenant). We have to kill the SS general. His name is . . . his name is von Kraut. He has a skull tattoo on his forehead and evil eyes. When he talks, everyone is trembling. Everyone but us.

"We jump off the plane in the dark," I whisper to my brother. "You are stuck in the tree. I take out a big, huge knife. Its blade is fifty centimeters long. It has a red star on the handle. The division commander gave it to me for my bravery when I saved his life. I already killed fifteen Germans with it. See the blood on the blade?"

"I take out my knife," he whispers back. "My knife is even bigger. Sixty . . . Seventy centimeters. And it has blood on the blade. And on the handle. The corps commander gave it to me for my bravery. When I saved his life and the life of his driver. I cut the strips—"

"Straps."

"Huh?"

"A parachute has straps. Not strips."

"OK. I cut the straps and jump down. I am the best jumper in the regiment."

"OK," I say. "The Germans come out on a tank and shoot at us. Bullets and shells swish in the air. You're afraid. You tremble. You hide behind a tree. You shoot at them, but your bullets ricochet off the tank's armor. I take out a grenade—"

"Baloney! I'm not afraid. I also take out a grenade. My grenade is bigger than yours. I throw it at the tank before you. Kaboom!!! The tank is broken. The Germans surrender. They cry like babies. I cut them down with my knife. I'm a hero."

That's too easy. If one grenade can do it, everyone would get medals and promotions. It's more complicated than that.

I say, "The tank is not damaged. You only scratched the paint. I throw my grenade and destroy it."

He sulks. "You always do this to me. I'm not playing anymore."

There is a word for guys like him. Black paper? Black male?

"OK. We did it together. Your grenade damaged the tank and mine destroyed it. And we take many prisoners. For each five prisoners, we will get a medal. We force them to sing The Internationale and dance the *kazachok*."

He's still not happy. "I want to sleep now," he says. "No *badya-bochki* or I'm gonna tell on you."

He's asleep faster than a kitten. I can't sleep. My mind is still on von Kraut. If we wait and kill him tomorrow, how many people will he murder today? What does he look like? He is probably dressed in black, is two meters tall, and wears shiny jackboots and a monocle. He probably has a German shepherd and a walking stick.

I get up and go to the window. It's spring now, and the windows are open. A mosquito buzzes by my ear. A cat walks by purposefully. He's gray even in the daytime. I can see our neighbor, Aunty Klava, across the yard. She's bathing Dasha in the portable zinc bathtub. They don't have running water either. Dasha goes to my school. She sits across the aisle from me. Her younger sister stands in her long nightie next to the bathtub, picking her nose. I can't see much through the half-drawn curtains, but my thoughts drift away from the SS general anyway.

My brother said that this younger sister showed him hers and he showed her his. They hid behind the shed and he promised not to tell anyone. I didn't believe that tale-spinner. He always makes things up.

"What did it look like?" I asked.

He drew it for me in the sand, an inhumanly perfect circle.

"You made it up," I said. "Or she tricked you."

"Honest," he said. "She said that she'll have sex with me during the summer break."

Right. He and honesty. Should I approach Dasha tomorrow and ask her if it's true about the circle? What is she going to lose? She is probably as curious as I am, and I won't tell anyone. And as for sex, I'll be careful. I don't want her to get pregnant. My brother doesn't understand that. He's too young.

Finally, Dasha emerges from the bathtub. I catch a glimpse of her buttocks, which are as skinny as mine. The lights go off across the yard. I wait for a few minutes just in case, and then return to my bed. My brother stirs in his sleep. Maybe he's catching up with von Kraut. Time to join him or he will get stuck again.

Tomorrow, I will know if girls really have perfect circles down there or is it a straight line as some boys in school say. But how about foreign girls? As super beings, they have got to be different. Maybe, like angels, they are above sex. Maybe they eat boys like my brother and me and spit out our bones. Will I ever find out if they are made the same way as the normal girls? When I wonder what Annie looks like naked, I blush.

But tonight, I'll take care of the general. I have no other choice. Someone has to protect the world against evil. My brother and I are chosen, and we'd be pussies to refuse the honor.

The Party

It's 1962. I am twelve. Today, my friends and I are forming the first Soviet Union's political party since the nineteen twenties. I will be the General Secretary, Petya Ogorodnikov will be the First Secretary and Fima Makagon will be another First Secretary. We will call our party the Party of True Goals. We will keep it so secret that no one in the world but us will know about it. But our Party will change the world for the better.

We hold our first session on a bench under a dying maple tree, a stone's throw away from the school gym. Someone carved the word *hui* into the bench's seat. To make sure that even people who cannot read understand, the carver added a crude drawing of a penis next to the word. We are careful not to sit on it. The ground is littered with cigarette stubs left by the teachers and the older kids.

"We can't have two First Secretaries," Fima says. "We can have one First and then the other will be the Second. Or the other way around."

Fima is a straight-A student. He's the tallest in the class, but he's thin like the intestinal worm they showed us in biology class.

"Yes, we can," I say. "I'm the General Secretary, and if I say we can, it means we can. If you don't like that, I will expel you and send you to Siberia."

"If we have the First and the Second, would you want to be the Second, Fima?" Petya asks. It's clear that he didn't get his A in history for nothing. He's shorter than me, and he's a freckled redhead. They taunt him like this:

Freckled, freckled ginger head
Your asshole is full of lead.

He got into a fight more than once because of that, and was called to the principle's office and his parents were summoned. He told me they spread some dry peas in the corner of the family room and forced him to stand there on his knees for an hour. He could barely walk after that.

It looks like Fima disagrees with Petya. He raises his hand and spreads his fingers. Each finger is a bone with a tightly stretched flap of skin around it. "See, one, two, three, four, and five. There is only a single one. Let's toss a coin." Fima has all As, including math.

"No coins," I say. "Tossing coins to make a decision is a bourgeois way of conducting business." I don't have an A in Marxism-Leninism for nothing.

"Here is what we are going to do," I say. "Fima will be the Secretary in charge of External Affairs and Petya will be the Secretary in charge of Internal Affairs. Deal?"

They nod.

"Now, let's see how we will change the world," I say.

"For the better," Fima adds.

"Let's make a law that all the boring subjects are dropped," Petya says.

"Let's make a law that there will be no wars," I say.

"Let's make a law that we all swim naked in the pool. Girls and boys," Petya says.

That's a thought. What would a naked girl look like? I've seen some reproductions in the art books, but reproductions don't jump into the pool next to you.

"We can't do that, Petya," Fima says. "Your *hui* is too small. The girls will laugh their heads off."

"My *hui* will grow when I get my girl," Petya says. "But you're a circumcised Jew. The foreskin never grows back. Even if all the girls in the class get naked around you."

Fima gets up. His face reddens. He makes fists, then turns around and leaves. I don't know what to say.

Petya shrugs, "But it's true."

It's true that his *hui* is small as well, but I don't want to press the issue.

At home, I tell my mother about the Party of True Goals.

"Why does it have to be a party?" she asks. "Call it a club or something like that."

That's a thought. If it's a club, we don't need to keep it in secret. We can enlarge our membership and invite a few girls. We will make them undersecretaries. I find the idea so funny that I laugh aloud.

"What did I say?" my mother asks.

"Nothing. I just remembered a joke."

"Tell me."

"It's an adult joke."

I go to the room I share with my brother. He's not here, which is good. I don't want the ten-year-old to pester me with some nonsense.

I lie down on the cot. A small party of ants is marching on the ceiling. They know what they are doing. They have a goal. A True Goal. They certainly belong to a club, but probably are not vice presidents.

I imagine all the girls in the class, even Natasha Beznos, naked by the pool. They all are stick figures or book pages below the necks. It's no use.

I should come up with a name for the club. How about the Club of True Goals? Clubs don't have secretaries. I will be the President, Fima and Petya will be the First Vice Presidents, and precious Natasha will be the Chief Treasurer. Everybody else will be members. Even girls. I laugh aloud again.

I shouldn't be laughing. This is serious stuff. Together, we will work hard, hand-in-hand, and change the world for the better. First, the Socialist Camp, and then the West. There is no truer goal than that.

The next day, in gym class, Petya drowns in the pool. Since we all roughhouse, no one notices until it's too late. Mr. Buga, the teacher, pulls Petya out. No one helps him. Petya's head, his ginger hair plastered to it, lolls while Mr. Buga carries him to a bench. We all stand around the still, limp body, while the teacher is trying to give him first aid. The girls hug each other and cry.

I've never seen a dead person before. Why did he drown? Maybe someone hit him or pulled him under? Maybe his asshole really is full of lead? But I can't believe he's dead. Maybe he's pretending. His open eyes stare at me. He might want something. What is his True Goal? Maybe he wants to be the Secretary in charge of External Affairs? Maybe he's sorry for what he said to Fima?

I look at Fima who stands right next to me. He's shaking, and his eyes are wet. The front of his swimming trunks is flat like a girl's. He's a pussy. I shrug. This is not happening. Just give Petya some time and he'll open his eyes and say something. Like, "Please, teach! Don't hit my chest anymore. It hurts."

Annie

It's 1966. I am sixteen. Father gets the third and last letter from Uncle Michael. Uncle writes that he works at DuPont, a chemical company. He lives in a three-bedroom house with a backyard, and goes to Florida every winter. He sends a photograph of his family. His hair is smooth now, but his grin is the same. His wife is big-eyed, as if it just dawned on her that she forgot to turn off the iron at home. Their three-year-old son, Lennie, is as serious as a Russian. Uncle Michael writes that the boy wants to be a millionaire when he grows up.

But the crown jewel is, of course, Annie. She is fourteen years old now, but looks sixteen. Every girl is a beauty to me, but Annie is a diamond among garnets. She's big-eyed like her mother, but looks self-assured. Her smile's like Mona Lisa's, only prettier. Above all, she's a genuine foreigner, born and raised. I can't take my eyes off her.

I tell myself that I will find Uncle Michael when I immigrate to America and ask him to teach me how to grin. And then I will marry Annie.

When Father leaves, my brother elbows me in the ribs. "Don't fall in love with Annie. She's your cousin. It's incest."

"Baloney," I say. "First of all, Uncle Michael is Father's cousin. That makes Annie our second cousin. It's perfectly OK. But then, who said I'm in love? She's just a baby. You're a pervert."

I photograph Annie's photograph, and always carry the copy around with me. In school, I project her mental image onto all the girls I used to lust after. They are not good enough to hold the train of her royal robes. From now on, whenever I meet a new girl, I compare her to Annie. They haven't got a prayer.

My father is writing his PhD thesis on machine translation. He's a revolutionary, and I'm very proud of him. Until now, only human beings could take a story in one language and make it sound alive in another. But it's a long and boring process for a translator, and it's expensive, too. When my father is done, it will be as easy and cheap as tuning your radio to the Voice of Moscow.

My father's field is English-to-Russian translation. He has no access to a computer, so his work is dull and manual. I help him collect some statistical data by counting how many times a given word appears in an English text. Say, how many times the word "and" shows up in a 1966 *New York Times* article on Elvis proposing to Priscilla. Twelve times.

My younger brother is recruited too, but he doesn't stay long. He has no patience for the job. He's too physical for this intellectual job.

My father doesn't promise me any rewards for helping. We are poor, you know that, he says. Worse yet, he smokes a cigarette now and then, the legacy of the Great Patriotic War, and I hate the smell. But just sitting next to him and checking off the appearance of a word in a notebook with a new fountain pen is a reward in itself. We are a team, two grown men on a scientific path. We are pioneers, father and son. That's glamour, happiness and satisfaction. I'm richer than any PhD. I'm richer than Elvis.

There is a question I have longed to ask my mother for years. I suspect that our father likes Volodya more than me. I'm ashamed to ask about it. To discuss family relationships, it's like discussing sex. It's not even taboo. It simply isn't done. Today I force myself to ask the question, indirectly.

My mother chops onions in the kitchen. I hate both the smell and the taste; my opinion is noted and overridden. I choose this awkward moment because it may mask some unwanted tears.

"Why is Daddy so stern, Mom?"

She's not turning to me. Her knife hand moves with the precision of a machine part.

"He lost his family in the Holocaust," she says. "You know this."

I do know. He lost everyone. His mother, his father, his brother and his sister. The Romanian Iron Guard, the Nazi's allies, killed them all. The neighbors said that they were rounded up one night and forced to march to a Romanian concentration camp. A neighbor, an Iron Guardsman, wanted to marry my aunt and save her. My grandmother said no. They died on the way to the camp from hunger and exhaustion. I saw their photographs. My uncle was my age.

"But you lost your aunt, too," I say. "And you're not so stern."

The last onion is reduced to slippery bits. She finally turns to me.

"He lost his *whole* family. And if everyone reacts the same as everyone else, life would be boring and predictable. Right?"

Yes, but why can't he react the way you do, I want to say, but I feel too uncomfortable to continue. Let it remain a mystery. I don't want any tears besides what the onions cause.

"Right," I say. "You convinced me."

Back to thesis work.

I'm looking for a few useful expressions along the way to supplement my high school English. They could be helpful conversation starters when I meet Annie, but I find none I can use. What would I do with the likes of "presents her with a ring he has purchased from his favorite jeweler, Harold Levitch, some time before?" So I have to make do with whatever they teach us in school.

"How old are you?"

"Who is your favorite writer?"

"Are you oppressed by capitalists?"

She'll say something equally witty, and, after that, things will go much smoother. I can't wait.

Entrance Exams

It's 1967. I am seventeen. Stalin is buried at last, and Khrushchev, the man who buried him, is denounced. I'm away from home, alone for the first time in my life. I'm a virgin. Tomorrow, I'll take my entrance exams at Moscow University's engineering school. I worry most about Marxist-Leninist philosophy. The rest is easy.

If I fail, I'll be conscripted. If I'm accepted, they will give me a deferment.

I want to study creative writing at the Literaturni Institute. I want to be a writer, sign my books in stores and talk on TV. I want women to beg me to autograph my books. I want to glide through the streets, smiling politely, and listen to people whispering behind me, "Alexander! Alexander! Isn't he great?"

But my parents want me to become an engineer.

"You can't make a living as a writer," my father says. "How many writers does this country need? You won't find a job. You'll be a Russian teacher at best. Do you want to be a teacher like your mother and me? On the other hand, an engineer always has his bread and butter. I wish I had your choices when I was your age."

"Teaching is fun," my mother says. "When kids learn something from you, that's happiness. But your father is right. Engineering is in demand by every society, which is a big plus in our turbulent times."

I don't want to be a teacher like my parents. Kids hate teachers. Teachers are miserable and weak. On the other hand, to control the flow of electrons in a wire or have the ability to calculate the speed of a meteor's descent to Earth is power. And I like butter.

I am like a Buridan's ass and an electron at the same time. I go for the closest stack of hay. I follow the path of least resistance. I hate my life.

Earlier today, I tentatively explored a few critical Moscow attractions: Red Square, the Kremlin, the metro, the Tretyakov Gallery, the Bolshoi Theater and the GUM department store. I was especially impressed by the Tsar Cannon inside the Kremlin, the biggest howitzer in the world. I've never owned a gun or didn't even know anybody who did, but being able to wipe out a horde of attackers with one shot is impressive.

I skipped the Lenin Mausoleum. That's not something I can do in a hurry if I could do it at all. It may be too painful for me. I'm not looking for pain.

Tonight, I'm looking for girls.

They glide hand-in-hand, in twos and threes, along the well-lit city's sidewalks. They giggle. They call each other those wonderful names. Katyusha, Ninochka, Natashenka, Olenka. Not as good as Annie, naturally, but still every name ends so softly, like the petal of a flower.

They smell like slowly ripening fruits. They are all rolling hills and hidden valleys. I've just recently discovered the highbrow word to describe them: nubile. It's an exotic, hot word. Nubile. Nubia. Labia.

If I raise my hands, I can touch them. That's why I won't raise them even if I need to scratch my nose.

You have to use a condom, my brother told me. Firstly, it's for your own protection. You don't want to know how many bacteria and microbes she has. Secondly, you don't want to knock her up because she and her family will force you to marry her. They call it a shotgun wedding though the family will use axes and knives.

He spoke in such a convincing, authoritative tone. He was fifteen. Another virgin. I nodded. No one would sell me a condom anyway. It's a tough-to-get thing. Maybe they use this type of plastic in the military, or maybe it's just not important enough. And even if they did sell them, I would be embarrassed to ask. Most pharmacy clerks are women. What if they ask me what size I need? What if someone else stands in line next to me?

Now, a plump redhead and a brunette pass by me. The redhead hits me in the ribs with her elbow. I apologize. I imagine taking their hands, leading them into the closest park, and having sex with both on the grass. It's not a concrete vision but an abstraction. Not images, but ideas. Not mechanics, but philosophy. I apologize again to their fleshy behinds. I construct apologetic poetry in my head, stanza after contrived stanza:

> *Oh, you beauty without measure,*
> *How can I repay you for my unintended assault?*
> *What can I sacrifice to your pleasure?*
> *If I may be so bold.*

They are long gone, but I still mouth the verses. The passersby probably take me for another drunkard. I am drunk. With love.

It's getting colder. A fierce northern wind gets under my sweater and into my thin cotton pants. They will lock the dormitory doors at 11 PM. When I descend underground on the escalator, only grim-looking men in gray fall clothing surround me. They look squeezed, dry and empty. I shudder.

I arrive before 11. The doorman, *vachter*, puts on his reading glasses and checks out my residence slip.

Later, when I sleep in the campus room full of other boys, I dream of the redhead and brunette sprawled next to me on red velvet sheets. They flaunt Rubenesque breasts, and their genitals are smooth patches of hairless skin without any traces of orifices. I reach out but they are gone. Instead, Stalin and Khrushchev appear.

"Why is dialectical materialism science?" Stalin asks, leaning against the wheel of the Tsar Cannon. Most of the muscles of his face have rotted away but his mustache remains. Khrushchev lights Stalin's pipe. He's balder than Humpty Dumpty.

I try to say something but I can't. I flail my arms, trying to buoy my way to the surface of the dream. A rough hand shakes me awake.

"You moan like a girl," a boy in the bed next to mine says. He has his flannel shirt on for warmth. The whiskers under his nose are sparse, like the grass in a Moscow park. I sit up in my bed and flex my muscles. He turns away, muttering under his breath. I don't think he recites poetry.

I lie down. "Motion is the mode of existence of matter," I whisper. Stalin would have been proud of me. So, too, would be the redhead and the brunette.

Virgin Dreams

IT'S 1968. I am eighteen. Earlier this year, the Prague Spring died under the tracks of my Fatherland's tanks. Beginning today, I wage the final assault in my private war against the internal enemy—my own virginity.

I stand 180 centimeters tall and weigh seventy kilos in my favorite striped boxers. Several girls have told me that I have beautiful emerald eyes and look like a starving artist. Others tell me that my shoulder-length raven hair frames my thin face as if I have just stepped out of a painting by Raphael. But none of them allow me more than a deep kiss and occasional breast-fondling.

Annie is too far away, so one of them will do. I hope she'll never find out.

In my coed dormitory, Strominka, located in the heart of Moscow, in the building that used to house Peter the Great's favorite regiment, *Preobrazhenski*, rumor has it that the spirit of an officer, clad only in a waistcoat and knee-length boots, roams the floors at night. They say that he is brave and bold, is afraid of no one: not of the administration that has powers to kick everyone out of the dorm, not of the sadistic cops who wear stars stolen from heaven on their shoulder boards, and not even of the all-powerful Chechen student union. They say that precluded from being politically correct by his upbringing in a regressive social environment, the spirit favors peeking at bathing girls in his quest for fun.

Some contemporary Strominka males cautiously follow his ghostly footsteps. The windows in the baths have been painted black by careless hands—paint peels off, and enterprising boys peep. If caught, they would be whacked by the girls armed with aluminum *shaikas*, the bathing pans used in traditional Russian baths, and expelled from school, which means mandatory conscription to the goose-stepping Armed Forces of the Soviet Union. But happier than a puppy chewing on a master's shoe, they continue to do their dirty deeds, and slap each other while exchanging juicy details later.

A famous poet visited Strominka and immortalized it in a verse.

> *When I am at Strominka,*
> *Snowflakes stick to my face . . .*

The day following my resolution, I sit on a bench in the courtyard, with my then-favorite book *Peter the Great* by Alexey Tolstoy in my lap, watching a real, live African prince stroll toward the Friendship Club like a lion on his way to a feast. The prince wears leopard-skin pants and a matching shirt, high-heel boots and a chain as thick as his bejeweled fingers. The ancient oaks shower him with gold leaves, and the Russian wind rustles his foreign hair.

Behind him, a plainclothed servant carries a huge drum. Muscles bulge on the servant's exposed forearms, and knots of veins pop on his neck, wide as a savanna rhinoceros'.

"Party time," a girl on the bench next to me says, addressing the empty space in front of her. Distracted, I missed her arrival. She has plump breasts under a tight sweater, long legs generously revealed by a miniskirt, shoulder-length hair of dark gold, and a fresh, round, snub-nosed face. She looks like *Snegurochka*, a fairy maiden made from virgin snow. Normally, a member of the Chechen student union, the rich and violent true rulers of Strominka, would claim her for a girlfriend before anybody else.

Actually, at this point, Chechens matter little to me, still a virgin at eighteen. I have sex in my dreams at least once a week, and have to go through the embarrassing process of washing my underwear in the dorm's bathroom afterwards, risking being seen by others, especially by a female janitor, a bulky loudmouthed woman in her fifties named Auntie Pasha the Hun.

"A professional band's coming. From their embassy," I say, watching the girl out of the corner of my eye. I have never been so bold, and I feel proud of myself.

She flinches as if seeing a ghost, and answers in a small voice. "Are you sure about the band?"

I get up, pulling down the too short sleeves of my old jumpsuit, and wishing I wore my prized possessions—East German–made blue jeans and an American checkered shirt where the second button from the top is replaced by a Russian one.

"A friend of mine overheard them talking," I say.

"He must've been nosy, your friend," she says, looking at me directly now.

"Do you mind if I sit down?" I ask. She shrugs.

Boys say that it means yes in girl-speak. I sit on the very edge, smiling tentatively in her direction.

"Today's their national holiday. Liberation day. They are from Muabiland," I say. She nods. Her perfume is overly strong, and I almost sneeze.

"What's your name?" I say and rub my nose. My cheeks are on fire.

"Olga," she says very softly, trying to pull her skirt over her knees. She fails by a few lovely centimeters.

"How are things in school?" I ask after clearing my throat. My voice still sounds hoarse.

"Fine, thank you."

"Do you like to dance?"

"Oh, yeah, I love to . . ." Her face lights up for an instant and she lets go of the hem of her skirt, but then her lips tighten again.

"If I ask you for a dance tonight, at the Club, will you dance with me?"

She blushes and then nods almost imperceptibly.

"Very well. I'll see you at the Club then. It's very nice to meet you." I run to my room, tips of my ears as red as the state flag when the sun shines through it.

My room, like the rest of the student rooms in Strominka, bears the heavy imprint of the barracks. There are seven metal beds covered with coarse woolen blankets; dressers, one for every two people; seven battered chairs; and a big square table used for dining, homework and even as a makeshift bed for an occasional illegal guest.

My English professor says that the word "dormitory" comes from the Latin "to sleep." I know that the Russian equivalent, *obshezhitie*, means "common living." While the English-speaking students sleep in their dorms, if they choose, their Russian counterparts, according to the creator of the term *obshezhitie*, can't afford this luxury.

Last year, when I was a first-year, I lived in an *obshezhitie* in the small village of Klyazma. I got up at six in the morning, careful not to wake up my roommates who were sleeping off last night's drinks, stood in line at the outhouse, shaved, got dressed, walked two kilometers to the train station while chewing on a liberally buttered bologna sandwich, took a 45-minute commuter train ride to the Moscow's Yaroslav station, rode a bus and the metro, and by eight, I was inside the lecture hall, fresh as a pickle forgotten in the back of a fridge. In the winter, I walked back to the dorm in the dark, by the piss-marked snow banks, listening to the howling dogs. In the summer, the drunkards lined up on the streets beginning at the Yaroslav station, and they entertained me with their songs and infighting until I hit the gates of the *obshezhitie*.

So now, I'm in dorm heaven.

Ignoring my roommates, I begin to rummage through my dresser, throwing things on the bed with the speed of a KGB agent in search of forbidden Western fruit.

"What's cooking?" Felix the Odessian, a skinny, black-haired fellow with watery eyes of an uncertain color, calls from his bed. He's fully dressed, even in his tie, holding a half-eaten chocolate bar in his hand.

"I've got a date," I reply proudly.

"Cool. You know how it goes; they are made of cookies and spice, and everything nice. With the help of a woman, we, men, multiply. I'll tell you a story on that subject—"

"Oh, please! Not again."

"OK. No stories." Felix throws the wrapper on the floor. His feet are on the bed's headboard. "But let me tell you something important. When a woman says no, she doesn't mean it. She wants to fuck as bad as we do, but she's afraid to be taken for a *davalka*, a promiscuous girl. That's why she says no. The most important thing for you is to sustain your erection. Remember that, my son, remem—"

"Shut up," my other roommate Vasily says, pushing away his textbook. He's older than the rest of us. His bushy mustache and sideburns make him look like a dashing hussar of Napoleonic wars. He just returned from serving in the army with a rank of sergeant. He was a tank commander, and an exploding Czech grenade gave him a concussion. Flexing his hundred kilos of muscles, he stares at Felix, who picks up the chocolate wrapper from the floor and quickly pockets it.

"You fellows have nothing to do," Vasily says. "In Czechoslovakia guys like you die left and right. And you have only sex on your minds. You should serve in the Army. They would make men out of you."

Felix mouths something behind his back.

Several hours later, I appear at the door of the Friendship Club, dressed in German jeans, an American checkered shirt, and a corduroy jacket, unbuttoned to show off a tie I borrowed from Felix.

"Be careful," Felix told me before I left. "If you get in a fight with the Chechens, make sure you protect your face. I don't want blood on my tie."

At the door, my senses are so assaulted by bright colors, excessively loud music, and seductive smells of perfume that I'm lost for a moment, unable to move. Somebody rams me in the back, and I enter gracefully.

I begin to push through the crowd, searching. That crowd is especially dense at the perimeters of the giant hall, leaving a bit of free room for dancing in the middle. But nobody's dancing yet.

Many foreign students come to study here, mostly East Germans or Africans. A few Poles, Bulgarians, and even Czechs are sprinkled here and there. They are elite people, even Czechs, simply because they are foreigners. They talk differently, they laugh differently, they dress differently, and they even smell different. They have better rooms. They have money. They are never sent to *kartoshka*, mandatory potato-harvest gathering. The girls love them, hoping to get married and become foreigners themselves. That is the nature of things, like the laws of physics that could be either liked or hated, but have to be obeyed.

At last, I see Olga, surrounded by a bunch of friends. She's dressed in something white, her neck and arms bare, and I'm too overwhelmed to notice more details. I get closer, but stay behind her, so she doesn't see me yet. I wait for the brave to start dancing.

The lights dim, the boys and girls holler, the band begins to play "Back in the USSR," and the first brave couple appears in the middle of the room. I shoulder my way to Olga, bow and ask, "May I have this dance with you?"

She extends her hand to me and smiles. Her perfume is different this time, much more subtle. We begin to dance, and time stops. We see nothing but each other. Not the frowning faces of the boys, not the envying faces of the girls. Nothing. The music halts and then begins again, but we don't stop, still half-embracing each other, still moving to the silent enchanted tunes of romance that play in our heads and our heads only. We whisper something to each other, without hearing the words. My hand on her shoulder is not mine anymore, and her shoulder is not hers. We are one being at that point of contact.

Suddenly, a heavy hand lands on my shoulder. An olive-skin man with an inky-black mustache under a curved nose says, "My turn," with a heavy Chechen accent. He's heavily pockmarked, just like Stalin used to be.

"Your turn to do what?" I say. I'm intoxicated with love and have lost all power of reason.

"To dance, dumbbell, to dance," the man says and increases his grip on my shoulder. His fingers are iron and his eyes are lead.

"I'm dancing with my boyfriend," Olga says.

"Who asks you, woman?" the Chechen says. He's breathing fire, like a dragon. The veins of his neck pop out as if about to burst and splatter the whole room with poison.

"Leave us alone," I say.

The man smiles. It's hard to concoct a less friendly smile than that. "You'll be sorry," he says and lets go of my shoulder.

Years or moments later, the music stops, the lights are on again. Holding hands, Olga and I begin to move through the crowd toward the doors.

"Hi, guys!"

I turn around briskly. It's Felix.

"Will you introduce me to your girlfriend?" he says and bows to Olga.

"Later, Felix, later," I say impatiently. But to get rid of Felix the Odessian is not that easy. Mere words would never deter him.

"You got to introduce me," he says, still smiling, showing off his gold tooth.

"OK. Olga, this is Felix Danchenko, my roommate. He's from Odessa, so you have to excuse him. Felix, this is Olga."

We make it to the foyer, and approach the entrance doors as rapidly as the crowd and Felix permit us.

"My pleasure," Felix says in the voice an English lord could have spoken in if he were born in Odessa. "Did you enjoy the band, Olga? Wasn't it—"

Suddenly his voice trembles, and he chokes. I follow his frozen stare, and see two olive-skin men, well lit by the flood lamps, waiting patiently outside. One of them holds an empty bottle by its neck. A cigarette dangles from his lips. His heavily pockmarked face is a mask of death.

I feel a sudden urge to urinate. Olga holds my right hand with a strength I did not expect her to have. I look back and see Felix disappearing in the crowd. I make a step toward the men and force a wretched smile.

"Hi, guys."

"Come closer, boy," the Stalin man says. "We want to teach you respect."

Another man comes from behind the Chechens, outflanks them in a dashing blitzkrieg and positions himself between the two armies. Vasily the hussar!

"Is there a problem?" Vasily says calmly. His hand is in his pocket. He probably holds a grenade in there or at least an Army knife with a 25-centimeter serrated blade.

The man with the bottle spits out his cigarette. "The boy has no respect."

"I'll take care of that," Vasily says, still holding his hand in his pocket, gazing unblinkingly on both men.

The men stare back. They're not convinced by either the grenade or the stare. The trumpets are about to call, the cannons are about to roar, and blood is about to get spilled.

But then a tall shadow appears on my left. It's a dashing officer in knee-length boots and a waistcoat, but his skin is transparent and peeling now, exposing bones and sinew underneath. His mouth is gaping, lipless. His eyes are mostly gone, except for the irises. A whiff of cold air touches the hot faces of the olive-skin men, making them shiver. I glance at Olga. Her eyes are fixed on the Chechens. I think she didn't notice the shadow.

"OK," the man with the bottle says and steps back. "We'll take your word for it."

Half an hour later, Olga and I get off the metro train at Sokolniki Park station. We emerge from the squat yellow exit in front of the park, successfully avoid a pair of wandering drunkards, a noisy all-volunteer citizen patrol and, most importantly, a huge gang of hoodlums engaged in their regular night stalking.

The park is colossal, extending for many kilometers. It's four times larger than London's Hyde Park. The tsars used to bring their falcons, *sokoli*, here to hunt hares and foxes. During the last war, the German patrols penetrated it, the closest to Moscow they ever got.

Olga and I find a dark and secure place under a tall elm, and kneel, facing each other. We are a pair of crafty foxes. No *sokoli* can find us here. I recite the poem in a dramatic whisper:

> *When I am at Strominka,*
> *Snowflakes stick to my face . . .*

Olga touches my lips with her finger. "Shhh . . ."

We kiss and lie down on the grass.

"My little berry," I say in the voice of an opera villain. My erection is testing the strength of my pants' seams.

The earth is cool, but at that moment, I feel as though I could heat up the entire planet with my body. She turns on her back, and I lean hard against her. The next few moments move too fast to be real or to be etched in memory.

"Is it over yet?" she says when we are done. "It's my first time. You know that, don't you?"

I know nothing. I kiss her. My stomach churns. I'm not sure what to say though I believe that some carefully placed words are mandatory. Guilt licks my heart with its raspy tongue. Will Annie ever forgive me?

"You are the best," I eke out. Good thing we can't see each other's eyes in the dark. Some things are better left unseen.

"You were marvelous," she says, staring at me with her unseeing eyes. "You're my knight in shining armor. You have beautiful emerald eyes."

Then she cries. I can't see her tears but I hear her sobbing. I'm ready to cry myself.

On the way home, we are silent. The night smells of flowers and leaded gasoline. The drunkards sing songs of death and procreation. Back at

Strominka, two Czech girls in bathrobes pass by us, laughing, heavy *shaikas* in their hands.

Auntie Pasha the Hun, who stands in the middle of the aisle, leaning on her mop, cheeks aflame from internal abominable fires, spits high-alcohol-content saliva on the freshly mopped floor.

"Jesus, those fucking foreigners," she rambles. "They're everywhere, everywhere."

I kiss Olga on the forehead at her door, and return to my room. The lights are off, and the boys are asleep. I undress and slide under the sheet. Strangely, my lips taste bitter. I'm tired, but too wound up for sleeping. I turn and toss, making the springs of my used mattress recoil loudly.

My roommates are grinding their teeth in their sleep or uttering shreds of words. I go to the window. It's the quietest hour of the night. The moon shines in my face, as bright as two hundred years before and, I hope, as bright as it will be two hundred years from now. A cool breeze rustles the remaining leaves, and twigs wave at me seductively like a bunch of *davalkas*. A new day, unstoppable, is rushing toward me. It will certainly be even nicer than the day it replaces. When I fall asleep, back in my bed, I dream of naked girls with *shaikas*, dancing around a ghost to an African drumbeat.

The Fighter

It's 1969. I am nineteen. I'm signing up for the karate class at my college, though the sight of a dozen sweating men fighting each other in pairs is nauseating to me.

Besides karate, I have the option of enrolling in a Sambo school. Sambo is a Russian martial art, an abbreviation of a word *САМозащита Без Оружия*, self-defense without a weapon. It's as good a martial art as any, but *karate* sounds much more exotic. Though it's not a Western word, it still has that irresistible foreign allure.

Back in high school, when I was sixteen, a boy named Ilya hit me right in the nose. It remains a bit crooked. Before the act of hitting, he asked me about my grades. He posited his question in the back of the school when I was on my way to take the city bus home. School buses were not in fashion at that time and that place.

I held a 5-kopek coin in my hand, ready to drop it into the bus' ticket counter. Sometimes I took an illegal free ride at the risk of being caught by a dreaded bus controller and ordered to pay a huge fine, but that day I had planned to be good.

I was surprised by Ilya's question. He was a year older than me, and the resident bully. Even teachers were afraid of him. Why were my grades of interest to a man like that? Yet I felt the need to oblige.

"Well, I got an A in History and an A in Math," I reported.

He nodded. I was glad he approved. Rumors had it that the best grade he had ever received outside of gym class was a C in History. He knew who Hitler was, and that had impressed the teacher.

Ilya nodded and then hit me. It was like a lightning bolt from the clear sky but not as loud. When I got up, he told me that he hated teachers' pets. I wiped off the blood. The back of my head buzzed from the contact with earth. I looked for the coin in the grass. Ilya didn't help me, and I didn't find it.

When the bus came, I sat in the back. The blood had stopped by then.

"What happened to you?" an older woman in the next row asked me.

"Nothing," I said. She had no need to know about my As.

But you can't just brush off an inquiring Russian woman. Especially if she's three times older than you, weighs twice as much, and is more motherly than a cat feeding her litter.

"Did someone hit you? A hooligan?"

"No. I fell."

"Poor baby. You need to put some ice on your nose. Or it'll grow crooked and no one will marry you."

I nodded, looking away. Did she think I carried an ice pack in my pocket? Besides, I had no time for alternative medicine. I had to be vigilant—every new passenger could be the controller. Sometimes they acted in pairs, entering the bus from both sides. I just wanted to be home. My parents were still at work, so if I could manage to sneak by my grandmother, I'd be OK.

"Why don't you take martial arts?" the woman said. "My son does and he's afraid of no one."

"Good idea," I said. "I will sign up tomorrow."

"Promise?" she said.

"Honest to Lenin," I said.

"What happened to you?" my brother asked me when I came home. He went to a different school, in the center of the city. It had the best teachers and the best students, just like him. Before we moved, when we both went to the same school, Volodya didn't do so well. During the 1st of May and November 7th demonstrations, his school was in the forefront. He carried the brightest banner, with a happy worker raising his hammer and a happy farmer raising her sickle. My school was last, and I carried the heaviest placard, with an American imperialist being bayoneted by a stern-looking Soviet soldier. My school stood on the outskirts of the city, among the rows of concrete apartment buildings called the Khrushchev Slums and single-story houses built the century before. Officially, the district was known as Korea, a name given back in the fifties in solidarity with our North Korean brethren.

I asked for a transfer several times, but my father said that I'd get better grades in my school and therefore higher chances for college.

"How about him?" I asked.

"He'd do well in any school," my father said. "You don't want to get conscripted, do you?"

Though my mother had explained his sternness, I never bought her explanation. There had to be something else. I couldn't ask him directly, of course. It just wasn't done. And as for my brother, I couldn't ask him either. He was my younger brother. I had a rep to protect. He couldn't possibly have a good answer anyway.

And as for my grandparents, to ask them was too embarrassing.

Maybe the head of the household had to be tough? Many, though not all, of my friends' fathers acted as if they were drill sergeants, though their relatives didn't die in the Holocaust. Maybe sternness was a sign of manhood? But still, not every grown man was tough. Was my grandfather tough to my father? Should I be tough to my future kids? Fortunately, I faced more pressing matters to dwell on.

My brother used to flinch when I raised my voice, but now he only scowls. He was taking boxing after school, and his friend Igor was the school's number one toughie.

"Nothing," I said. He had no need to know about my As.

"Want me to show you a good punch, Korea boy?" he asked. "Grandma's not home."

He is not circumcised. No one could do the circumcision in Siberia. He can take a leak with the other boys without being tormented.

"No," I said. I used to beat him up, but Grandma always saved him. She would shriek as if one of us hit her by mistake, and I always stopped. When she looked at us, there was so much love in her eyes that I forgot about pain.

It turns out that my college schedule is also busy, but I remembered my promise to the lady three years ago so I signed up yesterday, and I'm heading for my first lesson now. Ilya, wherever he is, should be trembling in his shoes.

Inside the smelly hall of the dojo, the instructor lines up a dozen boys against the wall. They all are about my age, except for one who, with his wrinkle-lined face, looks almost thirty.

"What are you here for?" the instructor asks. He's hardly older than us. No one replies.

He points his finger at me. "What are you here for, boy?"

"To learn karate, sir," I say.

"Why?"

"For self-defense."

He turns to the rest of them and laughs. "He needs to defend himself. Pussy."

Everyone laughs obediently. The instructor points to the boy next to me.

"And you?"

The boy snaps to attention. "To defend my country against the imperialists, comrade instructor!"

"That's it," the instructor says. "You've got it."

He pats the boy's shoulder whose ears are turning redder than ripe tomatoes.

We learn how to fall today. It's quite an art to land safely. The instructor kicks our legs out from under us and we land on the mats. No one falls better than me. It's an intelligent, artistic fall. Even the instructor admits that.

Where are you now, Ilya? I walk home very proud of myself, gliding over the wet asphalt and oil slicks. Both my brother and the woman from the bus would be proud of me. If you know how to fall correctly in my country, your future will always be bright and your relatives and strange women will get emotional over you.

The Artist

It's still 1969, and I'm still nineteen. I'm an engineering student and an aspiring artist. I want to be an artist not only because I'm creative (of course I am), but also because everybody likes artists. Everybody likes artists. Girls like artists. Even college professors like artists. So when I see an ad for extras for the Mosfilm movie studio, I know what to do right away. The homework and lectures can wait. Mosfilm even pays five rubles a day: glamour and money versus studies. This battle is so asymmetrical that there is no contest. I will sign up. Baby, I will be a star. I'll be Oleg Tabakov. I'll be Marcello Mastroianni. I pull the ad off the wall to throw off the competition.

The next morning, I take the metro to the studio. I stand in a long line of would-be stars. It's mostly young males, though there are a few grim-looking older women here and there. The movie bureaucrat examines my passport. Every institution in the Soviet Union wants to examine my passport. There is something in that little red booklet with the gold Soviet seal that attracts bureaucrats like gossipers to a freshly excreted scandal. He asks me about my movie experience. I have none. He asks me if I have epilepsy. I say I'm healthy as a horse. He asks me if I know how to shoot a gun. I say my father is a hunter and that he took me with him to shoot wolves and deer. Actually, I only saw wolves and deer in the zoo, but isn't this a place where they create make-beliefs?

I pass the interview. They give me a pass to show to the guard. I'll perform in the movie based on Bulgakov's play *Flight* about the Russian civil war. It looks like they took everyone, even the grim women. I will be a White Guard soldier, and the battle scene is huge.

In the book, several White officers committed suicide. They simply couldn't watch their world go down. Stinking gentlemen, refined sissies! A man should stand to the end and take a few extra enemies with him.

In the dressing barn, they give me a greatcoat, khaki pants, a tall, lambskin hat, and a rifle loaded with blanks. I still wear my own shirt because no one can see it under the coat. The hat has a white stripe pinned to it. The Reds have the same stripe, but it's, well, red. The barn has enough uniforms to dress a medium size army. I peek into the next room, and see shields, suits of armor, helmets, swords, bows and pikes for another horde. They have rooms for female clothing, but they won't let me in because women change in there. Their yells still ring in my ears half an hour later, after I opened the door. By accident, of course.

I know that they'll kill me in the end. But I'll still collect five rubles, enough to eat for two days and to pay for the metro fare. It's almost too good to be true.

In the book, the author quotes a nineteenth-century Russian poet Zhukovsky: "Immortality is a quiet, light beach . . . Have peace, he who finished his flight."

The grim women play nurses. I'd rather be shot to death than get treated by them. In the book, the leading women are young or exist only in the mind of one character.

I sit on the grass among my fellow White Guards and antediluvian cannons. We chat about foreign politics, chess, football and the weather. It's hot, but the woman in charge won't let us take off our greatcoats. They will start shooting any minute now, or so she says. She wears a summer dress and is equipped with a large bullhorn. If she were younger, she'd be attractive.

Finally, the camera rolls. The cannons roar. The Red Army cavalry unit comes over the ridge and bears down on us. Their sabers swoosh in the air. The man in the front carries a giant red flag. We shoot blanks at them. The sand from a fake explosion stings my cheek. The Reds rout us—kill most and herd the rest away. I lie dead, as I was told. I look at the bright sky and wish they gave us sunglasses. How did people fight on a bright day without sunglasses?

In the book, the White officers flee to Paris and Istanbul. Rumor has it that the movie crew will shoot some scenes there. How I wish I could go! I'd even take Istanbul. It's still an exotic foreign country. But they will hire the local extras, of course, though it will cost them precious hard currency. The Russian extras could defect. And to prevent them from defecting is far more important than saving a few dollars or pounds.

Later, I stand in line to collect my five rubles. My cheek still stings but a movie star pays no attention to small discomforts. Most extras are already in their civilian clothes but one man, still dressed as a Red Army horseman, cuts through the line. People shout at him but he moves ahead. A boy behind me says that the Reds get ten rubles a day because as equestrians they are more qualified than the rest of us. They also get to see new movies for free between shooting scenes. Ten rubles a day is 200 rubles a month if you don't work Saturday and Sunday. When I graduate as an engineer, I'll get 120 rubles a month. If I'd get ten rubles a day, I wouldn't need to graduate. Eighty more rubles, stardom, free movies and a shiny saber. What more could a man possibly want?

In the book, some White officers returned to Red Russia from Paris. No Soviet person would ever do that. First, Paris is way too romantic. Second, most Whites who returned home were killed or arrested. They were naïve and we are not.

On the way home, I notice girls look at me. Just this morning, not one of them paid any attention. It seems like the movie business put an indelible mark on me. I wish I could meet Annie now. When I finally check my cheek in the mirror, I discover why they looked. The cheek is dirty and bloody. It's an extra's cheek. It's a defeated soldier's cheek. That's OK. So what if I get an F tomorrow? That's also OK. One of these days, I'll learn how to ride a horse, and they will promote me to a Red Army horseman. Then all the girls will be mine, and I'll cut to the head of the line any time I want to. And then I will go to Paris. That's La Dolce Vita. No one, but no one, will take flight from that.

Bitter Almonds

It's 1970. I am twenty. Comrade Orlov meets me at the gates and motions me to follow him. For the next month, I will cling to him like an electron to an atom nucleus, and will depend on him like a fish in an aquarium. The guard examines my papers, making sure that the Cyrillic letters of the stamp say what they are supposed to, and that the black-and-white shot on the ID matches my face. He doesn't check Comrade Orlov's papers. It's hard to forget Comrade Orlov once you've seen him. He is taller than my 180 centimeters by a head, and his shoulders are wider than a garage door. His teeth are stainless steel.

Comrade Orlov moves along, indestructible as a Hazmat truck. I follow. My rubber-booted feet propel me over brilliantly red and green puddles and over wet dirt that makes a sucking sound every time I pull them out.

People who work at the Sunshine Chemical plant, the leading producer of industrial plastics for the Red Army, are mostly *zacks*, condemned criminals serving their sentences, but Comrade Orlov is a free engineer. He will be my boss, mentor, and advisor for the next month. This is my practice study, mandatory for graduation. I can't become an engineer in my own right without it. We walk silently. The place is surrounded by a chain-linked fence topped with barbed wire. Overhead, the metal pipes, thin and wide, criss-cross each other like the doodling of a lunatic.

The complex cacophony of smells makes me cough, though in my four years of studying chemistry, I'm used to harsh odors, spills and even explosions. A few steps later, I pick up a smell different from the rest.

"Some kind of a nutty smell, Comrade," I say. "Bitter almonds?"

"You're right, student. It's hydrogen cyanide. Used in the production of acrylic plastics, nylon, cyanide salts, lactic acid, nitrates, chelating agents, dyes and pharmaceuticals, as you well know. The pipe is rusty. No money to fix it."

I nod. I just finished reading Dante's "Inferno," so I recognize Hell right away. I've abandoned all hope. I'll be lucky to get out of here alive.

We arrive at a grim, mustard-colored two-story building. He leads me into a tiny office and points me to a wooden desk. The periodic table of elements is attached to a wall with pushpins. There are gas masks and Hazmat suits. A rusty, disassembled chemical flow controller, its pipes sticking out like the legs of an octopus, its dials round mollusk eyes, occupies half the desk. Books are stacked up on each other.

"Here is the list of hazardous materials used at this plant," Comrade Orlov says. "Study that first. That and the evacuation plan." Then he leaves. I am alone in the office. I hear muted voices and the familiar hum of lab equipment behind the partition.

I study the list. It's as long as the line for milk in the productive Soviet society. I read about cyanide twice: "Acute exposure can result in symptoms including weakness, headache, confusion, vertigo, fatigue, anxiety, dyspnea, and occasionally nausea and vomiting." When I'm done, I check out the evacuation plan. In a nutshell, it advises you to put on a white sheet and crawl to the closest cemetery. Then I examine the controller and sketch out its parts in a notebook. The controller smells of formaldehyde. A few lines of witticism and a star with a hammer and sickle inside are carved into the rough surface of the table. I trace its contour with my finger. Tomorrow, I will bring a penknife. I can carve a monster or two of my own, and I'm full of witticisms. Man is woman's best friend. The Beatles are gods. The brain tramples the heart.

I peer out of the window but see no people other than an elderly *zack* in his gray cotton pants and jacket who is hammering at a pipe in a slow, indifferent pace. He has to be a Flatterer from the Eighth Circle. He lifts his eyes to me. They have no whites.

Later that night, I return to the dorm I'm housed in. I share the room with two other students from two different schools, Petruha and Boris. I haven't had a chance to talk much to them because I arrived late yesterday, unpacked my suitcase, introduced myself, shook hands and went straight to bed. They talked to each other about a fight they'd been in at the cinema, and for the next few minutes while I was balanced between dream and reality, I also kicked and hit and was kicked and hit like them at the entrance to a dance floor or in a movie theater foyer, or maybe in the alley behind a grocery store. Boris and Petruha have different advisors. This is a big plant.

Now, when I enter the room, they sit at the table over the typical student fare—picante sandwich: white bread with mayo, a cut onion and a few slices of cut cabbage that, according to health gurus, calms people down before exams. There is also a bottle of clear liquid and a few glasses. I suspect it's not water.

"Want some?" Petruha asks. He's shorter than me but wider in the shoulders. His dark hair falls on his pimpled forehead. He is growing a mustache under his bulbous nose. "It's pure alcohol. I took it at the plant."

I take the proffered glass, take a gulp and smell my sleeve, as the experienced drinker should. The sleeve smells of formaldehyde and bitter almonds. I grab the picante sandwich and take a bite. It tastes like cardboard.

"Atta boy," Boris said. He looks like a *rynda*, a squire-bodyguard at the tsar's palace: very erect, round-faced, rosy cheeks, long blond hair parted in the middle. Give him red boots, a calf-length white coat, a tall white hat, a ceremonial silver ax, and he would be ready to stand behind any Russian ruler.

"Wanna go dancing?" he asks. "They got cool girls here. Hair bleached by acid."

The three of us take a bus to the dance hall. We wear big-buckled soldiers' belts for weapons. The bus is full of workers returning home. They mostly stare into space, smoking, stinking of sweat and chemicals, but one, a gorilla of a man, is singing the old sailors' song "Yablochko." He has probably forgotten the words because he doesn't go beyond:

> *Little apple,*
> *Where are you rolling?*
> *You'll get into my mouth*
> *And will never come back.*

His voice is good though it's roughed up by smoke. The *zacks* are driven in their own buses. I wonder what they sing and what they do in their spare time. Probably play chess.

We buy our dance tickets at the entrance to the hall. Inside, flocks of boys and girls criss-cross the floor without touching. The band plays "Yellow Submarine." The lead screamer looks a bit like John Lennon. He's equipped with a pair of round glasses, only his cheekbones are more prominent than John's, his skin is that of a Turkish minority and his jeans are Polish-made.

We cut into one girls' flock and ask the three of them for a dance. I know that my confidence, which I have artificially boosted with those few gulps of alcohol prior to coming here, won't last too long, so I invite the closest one. The girls say yes to Boris and me, but no to Petruha. His face turns dark. "In my village," he says to the girl who has refused him, "we spank the girls for that. With a belt."

I don't know what her reply is because I dance away. The girl is tall and supple. She wears a sexy summer dress. Her long hair is held by a plastic hoop. Her nose is too upturned for my taste. I am certainly too good for her, but she is a female. Francesca da Rimini. My hand is on her back and hers is over my shoulder. My heart gives my ribs a beating.

If I close my eyes, I may be able to imagine that she is Annie. Until she talks.

"What's your name?" I shout over Lennon's amplified voice.

"Valya," she shouts back. "You're a student?"

It's not as romantic as Francesca or let alone Annie, but will suffice. I'm careful not to stomp on her foot, and we gyrate. When we are done, I escort her back. Petruha is still there, his hands in his pockets, brooding.

"Come on," I say to him. "Look how many girls are here. You're a student. You can get anyone you like."

"I wanna teach the broad a lesson," he says. "It's a matter of honor. Don't you understand honor, huh?"

Valya-Francesca pulls me by the hand. "Come on, let's have another dance."

Half an hour later, we are outside. "You're my little apple," I say to her. "My Beatrice." We kiss. My hand travels down her spine.

I hear screams and break away from Valya's inviting lips. I see Petruha spinning his belt over his head like a sling while two boys with broken bottles advance at him.

"Excuse me," I say to Valya, pulling my belt out. Good thing my pants are tight on my hips. She smiles at me and unbuttons her blouse. I freeze, feeling a stupid grin parting my lips. But then I hear the cops' whistles, and we run. I hold her hand at first, but soon lose her in the crowd of stompers.

Back at the dorm, Boris is on the bed, kissing his girl. I leave. The building is only one block away from the plant, which shoots plumes of rainbow-colored smoke into the night air. Music plays. Something lyrical, from World War II. The Great Patriotic War, as we call it. A man takes a leak against the side of the building. There is no place for me to go. I circle the building. I sigh. I go back inside and sit next to the doorman, who is a woman. Aunty Nastia. I already have shown her my pass enough times to satisfy a bridge-guarding troll, but she asks for it again. I show it to her. I'm easy.

"Why do people fight, Auntie Nastia?" I ask. "Why can't they get along? Imagine a brotherhood of man, if you can."

She looks at me as if I were a talking ant. She's old. Over forty for sure. Her eyes are sunken in and her face is criss-crossed by wrinkles like the French earth in World War I. No, she's fifty, at least. An ancient woman, full of experience. Maybe she can dispense words of wisdom, like a Himalayan guru.

"So, why, Auntie Nastia?"

Her eyes light up. She opens her mouth, a cavern in a mountainside. Stalactites and stalagmites are growing inside it. Her tongue is a serpent that dispenses wit.

"Go back to your room, punk," she says. "Or I'm calling the cops."

She's not a guru. She's is a False Counselor from the Eighth Circle of Hell. I crawl upstairs like a kicked dog, which I am, and sit on the wooden floor by the door to my room. It's quiet inside, but I still don't dare to enter. I close my eyes and fall into a half-dream. I see myself running the length of a tall fence, a pack of dogs in close pursuit. I wake up when someone shakes my shoulder, and it's not a dog. It's Petruha. His hand is wrapped in a bloody towel.

"What's going on, pal?" he asks.

I get up. My left leg is still asleep.

"It's Boris," I say. "He's making out with a girl."

Petruha sits down at my feet, extracts a cigarette from his pocket and lights it up. I notice that he has round, fishy eyes.

"What happened?" I ask, pointing to the hand.

"Nothing," he says. "Just a cut. Will heal before I marry."

"Does it hurt?"

"Not much. But I hit one of them good."

I don't dare press for details. I slide down along the wall and sit next to him. He offers me a cigarette but I refuse. He delivers me the details anyway, between the puffs of smoke. Two guys tried to cut him with broken bottles. He whacked one in the forehead. The other pulled out a knife. Petruha hit him on the fingers. He ran away.

Finally, the girl emerges from the door. She walks away slowly. We stare at the liquid movement of her hips and whistle. She turns and sticks out her tongue at us.

Boris is in bed, wearing nothing but a satisfied grin. "How was the dancing, guys?"

"You're one sick fuck," Petruha tells him. "I have cramps in my ass because of you."

I settle to read a textbook. Petruha sulks in the corner, muttering curses under his breath. The bare bulb, hanging from the ceiling on the wire, paints everything yellow, as if we have the life of ease and live in a submarine.

When I finally get into my bed, I can't fall asleep for a while. What if the dogs of my previous dream catch up with me? I don't remember if I wore my belt in that dream. If I did, I would feel much better. Finally, my eyes close and I begin to drift toward the dogs. Just as they appear, I hear a muted explosion somewhere deep in the guts of Hell, which is the next block over. No alarm sounds, and who cares about someone shouting outside. Another man, drunk as a fish in a polluted puddle. Another tormented soul, even if he sounds just like Mr. Orlov. Tomorrow is another day at the office. I can't be bothered.

Boris and Petruha stir in their sleep, burying heir heads deeper into their shriveled, anorexic pillows. I drift into my sleep, and the whiff of bitter almonds slowly enters the room through the wide-open windows.

Shalom Aleichem

It's 1971. I am twenty-one. This is normally a quiet street, just half a mile from Red Square and the Kremlin. A few overweight mothers in flowery cotton dresses push rusty-wheeled carriages. An occasional drunk curses under his nose. An old woman in a babushka leans on a cane, an *avoska*, a string bag full of groceries, in her other hand. A school of juvenile hooligans floats to-and-fro. Flatbed trucks, buses, and a few exhaust-belching Ladas rumble by. It is a typical day in Moscow.

But now, on this clear October day during the Jewish holiday Simchat Torah, the cops close the parallel streets and direct all traffic through this street, Ulitsa Arhipova. Because Moscow's oldest synagogue, with its classical façade and colonnades in the front, is located here, and because the Jewish youth come here once a year. From what I know, young Jews don't care for other holidays, but this one seems to be youth-oriented. The government can't allow the opium of religion to cloud young minds, of course, hence the traffic switch.

I don't know what other kids are here for, but I come to check out what Simhat Torah is, and, as an important side business, to pick up girls. I've been to an Orthodox church once, and found it too theatrical for my taste. Too much gold, too many elaborate robes, too much singing in Old Russian.

I didn't know how to get to the synagogue, so, as my friend and roommate Tolyan advised me, I followed the noses from the metro station to the synagogue. "Jewish noses are bigger and look like a hatchet," he said. He is Jewish, but his nose is not any bigger than mine. And it's straight like a bowie knife's blade.

"Let's go together," I told him earlier today while I was shaving with my precious electrical razor. "It's gonna be fun."

"I can't," he said. "I'm graduating next year. I'm afraid they'd kick me out if I go. We Jews are cowards. I can't help it, but I'm always in the majority. You know that, right? You are Jewish yourself, right?"

Now, I stand on the other side of the street, surrounded by Jews, who are only a few here if you judge by their noses, and, using the Biblical expression, by the mixed multitude, which consists of KGB agents, plainclothes policemen, onlookers and a few guys who came here to pick up girls. I wear my best clothing: Polish-made jeans, Yugoslav platform shoes, a cowboy shirt, and a patent-leather jacket.

I like the way the girls look. They are tall and thin and soft-skinned and big-breasted, and their noses are as if they were drawn by a ruler, all of them, without exception, Jewish and from the mixed multitude. Boys outnumber them two-to-one. One boy in a yarmulke shakes my hand. "My name is Uriah," he says. "It's from the Bible. It means *The Lord is Light.*"

He shakes hands with everyone. He's lying, of course. His name is probably Uri. No one in the Soviet Union can be named Uriah, unless he was born before 1917. No one gives their children a religious name in the Soviet Union.

Uri sings a Jewish song and everybody follows. It's easy, because there are only two words in it, "shalom" and "aleichem." It means "peace be upon you," Uri explains. The Ladas and trucks honk. The drivers shake their fists on us and shout curses. They don't want peace. Soon, they will throw bottles. It's hard to miss in such a dense crowd. And if they hit an agent, too bad. As Stalin used to say, "If you cut wood, don't worry about splinters."

The sun disappears behind the buildings, rolls toward Poland and then the evil West. Maybe it will complain to the UN once it reaches America. The breeze lifts dust and shreds of *Pravda* that escaped its usual fate as ass-wipes. The synagogue is full, but I manage to peek inside. What I see makes little sense to me. Bearded men in white, fringed prayer shawls rocking in place, singing out of synch without any music accompaniment in a language I don't understand. There is no sign of women. From what little I know, they might be upstairs, behind the partition, hidden from the prying eyes. They are probably old anyway.

The young ones mix with the boys outside. Though the hall is elaborately designed, the atmosphere is less theatrical than in the church but not less confusing.

Someone slaps me on the back. I turn to face a boy I'm sure I've seen somewhere. His nose is hooked but looks more Georgian or Armenian than Jewish. As we say in Russia, a Caucasian, which, unlike in America, means a native of the Caucasian mountains. But who am I to tell? Unlike the late Joseph Stalin, I'm no expert on nations.

"If you want to graduate from college," the boy says, "leave right now and never turn back."

"Huh?" I say, studying his face. He looks confident but not friendly. He is not a well-wisher. He obviously doesn't speak on his own authority. He's obviously a plainclothesman. I wish I could say something witty. Like, "Who the hell asked you, Jew?" Or, "How much do they pay you? Thirty silver rubles a head?"

"You heard me," he says. His eyes are as prunes oversoaked in the sun. I should kick his ass, or, as we say in Russia, tear off his muzzle. I'm sure Uriah will help. Together, we will take the snitch apart. Stoning him would also be good. Crucifying is not an option. No time.

Instead, I turn away and leave without a girl and without learning about Simchat Torah. I want to graduate and to work at a chemical plant to build medicine for my people. I want to get married to a tall, thin, soft-skinned and big-breasted girl, no matter if her nose is or is not drawn by the ruler. But above all, I want to leave the country to a place where no KGB agents generally lurk in the mixed multitude and where everyone worships what he wants, from Buddha to Mammon. I'm a coward who can only mutter "peace be upon you," instead of kicking ass.

It's quieter around the corner. The hatchet-noses are gone, the sun has already set, the cars are few, and streetlights throw circles of semi-darkness on the pavement. I pass a bronze Lenin. He clutches his proletarian cap in a grip so tight that it would take years of hard work to force it open. Come to think of it, I do love hard work. Maybe Tolyan is wrong. Maybe Jews are not cowards. I turn back. I'm ready to tear off muzzles. Annie would be proud of me.

Warriors

IT's 1972. I am twenty-two. The air is dead inside the barrack in the town of Kineshma, to the north of Moscow. Nothing dead ever moves unless something moves it, and the only way to move the air around is by fanning yourself with the newspaper *The Red Star*. The newspaper has another useful purpose, considering that toilet paper is in short supply. Outside, the air is alive, stirring the tops of the birches and caressing the hair of the Kineshma girls in the street. The sergeant won't let us out either. Maybe he's afraid for our innocence. Maybe he fears that we will catch diseases. Maybe the citizens of Kineshma complain. Maybe he envies us. Maybe he's a jerk.

The sergeant's eyes, tiny and indestructible, sit deep inside his face as if someone hammered them in with the barrel of a rifle. His forehead, prominent cheekbones, and flat nose with a red-and-white pimple on the top are covered with sweat. His jackbooted, bow legs are designed to hug a horse's back. His powerful hands are designed to hold a curved sword and a leather-bound shield. A steel-buckled uniform belt cuts his short figure in two. Everything below is ugly and stupid. Everything above is stupid and ugly.

Behind him, a portrait of Brezhnev sprouts on the wall. If Stalin's most prominent feature was his mustache, then Brezhnev's are his eyebrows. They weigh the same, gram for gram, whisker for whisker. A Russian saying, "you crawl on your eyebrows," means that you're drunk. Brezhnev looks like he mastered the art of speed crawling. He could have been an Olympic winner if that was a sport. I would cheer him on.

"The American imperialist soldier wears socks. Question: why does

a Russian soldier wear his *portyankis* wrapped around his feet?" the sergeant asks, pointing to a piece of a soft flannel in his right hand. His
Tatar accent is harsh. "Answer: they dry faster and serve longer than
socks. Understand? That's why we're gonna win World War III. With
portyankis and Russian ingenuity."

"But they are notoriously hard to put on, Comrade Sergeant," I say.
I sit in the first row. I always do. I get the spittle from the speaker, but I
won't miss anything useful.

The hammered eyes circle the room and train on me. "Get up! Question: did I give you permission to speak, private?"

I get up. Sweat trickles down my neck. It's thirty degrees inside. Cel-
sius. And it smells of the sweaty *portyankis* of thirty men. Probably the
battlefields of Verdun smelled like that.

"Answer: no, Comrade Sergeant."

The finger of the sergeant's *portyankis*-free hand points to my face.
Its nail needs trimming. I wish I could bite it off and spit it back in his
face.

"Are you getting funny with me, private?" he asks. His eyebrows are
sparse and faded. That's what you get for crawling on them for too
long.

"No, sir." I'm not getting funny. I'm always funny. That's what I am.
I can't help it. Can't you see this, you moron, you sweaty Tatar with a
grade-school diploma? Answer: I'm funny. Understand?

"Then shut up and listen," he says. "Understand?"

"Yes, sir." I stand at attention. I hope to drown him in my sweat. I
hope my *portyankis* stink will suffocate him before he gets a chance to
put on his gas mask. I hope he will drop dead from old age. He's probably pushing forty.

"Do you need a special invitation to sit down, private?"

I sit down.

"Get up! Shame on you, private. You're a student, gonna be an engineer soon. You'll be a reserve officer. What kind of officer will you be?
What will you teach your subordinates?"

I get up. When I am an officer, I'll order you to crawl from here to
Moscow. With the full pack. On your eyebrows. That will teach my
subordinates how to be fit.

"I don't know, sir!" I say.

"Who ordered you to sit down?" the sergeant asks.

I contemplate the fate of us comedians. Some people like us, but we never get to be presidents, emperors or Party secretaries. That's why the petty bosses persecute us, knowing too well we will never repay them later.

"You did, sir," I say when I finish contemplating, a second later.

A few minutes later, I'm doing my push-ups outside, in the shade of the birches. I can see the girls from here through the iron gates, and the boisterous air cools off my face. If the sergeant will let us, we'll go to the dance club tonight. Even the provincial Kineshma girls like comedians. Especially future engineers, officer cadets, Moscow students, the defenders of the country against the American soldiers in socks. And we can get into a fight with the local boys. Steel-buckled belts are almost as good as curved swords.

I pause. The sergeant is gone. I'm free until he returns. I hug the warm earth and it hugs me. I'm immortal.

Dutch Interiors in

the Age of Reason

IT's 1972. I am twenty-two. In Russia, it's honorable to argue with a tour guide. A sophisticated, pointed argument makes it clear that you are more knowledgeable in the subject than he is and that your balls are bigger. After winning, you walk tall and proud, and girls' admiring glances stick to you like leaves from the massage brooms they use in the Russian steam bath, and everyone showers you with attention.

"It's on loan from the Met," the tour guide says, pointing to Johannes Vermeer's *Young Woman with a Water Pitcher*. "The Met is a museum in America."

The guide is a man in his forties, with the head of Rodin's *Thinker* attached to the body of a former wrestler. If he bangs his head accidentally, it might fall and roll on the floor. Wouldn't that be cool?

"Vermeer's paintings often feature women in domestic interiors," the guide says.

"You should say Ver-me-er, not Ver-mir," I correct him.

"The woman's attire indicates her elevated social standing," the guide says. His lips are twitching. Maybe he is new to this business? Then it's my social responsibility to teach him.

"You've got this right for a change," I say, stressing the word "this." "She holds a silver pitcher."

He turns to me. His eyes are red. He needs some rest. He needs to get laid. He needs a better job. Perhaps a winning lottery ticket would take care of his problems. Naaah. He is a lost case.

"Let me talk first, comrade," he says, "and then you can talk. How does that sound?"

I want to say that his voice sounds a bit too shrill. I want to say that I don't like the way he stressed "comrade." I want to say that he is not the boss here.

"Sure, sure," I say. I'm not the confrontational type.

I approach an attractive girl about my age, and tell her, "I read a novel about Vermeer. I got a headache this big because it was in English."

She gives me a sideways glance and returns her attention to the guide. I shrug. She is too timid for me, and her nose is too long. Her dress is too tight and that pimple under her nose—bleh! Who in the world would call her attractive? She's not even a pale shadow of Annie. Just an invisible shadow.

"He painted only about thirty-five works," the guide says.

"Thirty-four," the girl shouts. From the way she pronounces her Os, I can tell she's not from here. Probably from the Volga region.

"It's actually thirty-six," I say. She looks at me, clearly admiring the breadth of my knowledge, intelligence, and manliness. Her eyes are blue, the color of the dress in the painting. If you look closer, her nose is fashionably patrician, the pimple is barely noticeable, and the tight dress makes her breasts look cool.

I will buy her lunch, I think. I'll insist, even if she would want to go Dutch.

"I want you to leave," the guide points at me.

"Bullshit," I say. "I paid three rubles!"

"Right," the girl says to me. "He has no right to kick you out!"

I will date her, I think. She has balls. Breasts and balls. Vermeer would love to paint that. Or was it Bosch who liked bold chicks? Maybe Rembrandt? No, Rembrandt's chicks were conventional females, if fatty.

The guide looks as if he is ready to bang his head against the wall.

I turn to the girl. "Let me show you the next hall," I say. "They have Rembrandt in there. He did several hundred paintings."

She takes my hand.

"Three hundred and fifty," she says and sticks her tongue out at the guide.

Maybe I will marry her. We will live long, and we will prosper, and we will have many ballsy kids who will be able to tell Bosch from Vermeer as well as the best guide. But in addition to the rules of verbal engagement, I will have to teach them to keep their emotions in check. Take it from me—that's the reasonable thing to do in this age.

Half an hour later, I change my mind about marrying her. She's simply not a good listener. I spill my soul for her, but she acts like Vermeer's *A Woman Asleep at a Table*. It's a betrayal of trust.

I tell her that "ever" is a too emotional word when it's chained in the middle of "happily" and "after."

"What the hell it means?" she says.

"I rest my case," I say. Forty-five minutes after we met, we drift apart like two chunks of ice in the ocean. That will teach me to stay cool with women.

The Train on Its

Way to Derailment

It's 1973. I am twenty-three. I just graduated from college, and am heading for my first job at Yoshkar-Ola, an Eastern city I've never heard about until a few months before. I take a bus to the train station. The rain has been pouring since early morning and by the time I arrive I'm soaked. Not to the bones yet, but it's getting under my skin. I climb aboard the Yoshkar-Ola bound train.

In my sleeping compartment, I find two sets of narrow bunk beds of hardwood five feet apart. A small table sits between the bunks and a blinking fluorescent lamp on the ceiling casts a greenish tint on the faces of passengers: a young couple, probably in their early twenties, and a uniformed Navy lieutenant, also the same age.

I introduce myself, and we shake hands. I land next to the Lieutenant. The woman proudly announces that she is in her fourth month.

"I hope it's a boy," she says. "I wish the doctors did the tests. Like they do in America."

"They do everything in America," her husband says and blows his nose into a checkered handkerchief. "They have everything in America. You name it—they have it."

"I wish I knew ahead. I would have an abortion if I knew it is a girl," the woman says. "My firstborn has got to be a boy."

She has a round peasant face with an upturned nose and healthy rosy cheeks. Just like a *matreshka*. I expect her top half to come off and expose another doll inside, just like her, but a trifle smaller. She wears a modest flower-patterned dress, ankle-length, with a white collar, dark cotton stockings and black patent leather pumps.

"A real man is always clean-shaven and slightly drunk," the Lieutenant says and laughs. "Let's celebrate."

He pulls a bottle of vodka from an ancient wooden suitcase with brass corners. There are two faded stick-on labels on its side. One says Paris and the other, Berlin. The Lieutenant's expressionless face seems to be carved out of a flesh-colored stone. A deep vertical crease cuts his forehead in half.

"That used to be my father's," he says, pointing to the suitcase. "And before that, it was his father's. My grandfather took it to the War. It traveled all the way to Berlin."

The Lieutenant's head is cleanly shaven, which make his ears appear half the size of an elephant's. He has a bunch of spit-shined medals pinned to his uniformed chest, and they jingle when he moves. His neck is thin, with a couple of razor nicks. A few zits shine prominently on his cheeks.

"This one's for Czechoslovakia," he points to the biggest medal, intercepting my gaze. "Those Czechs gave us quite a fight. One guy threw himself under my tank. He had hand grenades in both fists. Good thing they didn't go off. He was flat as road kill when we ran over him."

He pauses for a good, hearty laugh. His eyes don't laugh. It seems like the sound of his voice intoxicates him. My stomach churns. I've never sat so close to a confessed killer.

"You're a hero," the husband says.

"If not for the Soviet Union," the Lieutenant says, "if not for the people like us, the Socialist Camp would go down the drain. Like . . . Like a train on its way to derailment."

I half expect that he'd jump to his feet, raise his right hand at a forty-five degree angle, put the other hand on his crotch and begin shouting slogans. One day he'll be a Party boss.

"My ship goes to Sweden often," the Lieutenant continues. "Nice country!" At this point, he nods, approving his own words. "Everything's for sale. I had a girlfriend in Stockholm. A real millionaire's daughter. A capitalist swine, heh-heh-heh. But a beautiful, gorgeous girl, like in a fairy tale. I've often thought why she dated me. I think because she was always bored. And I was different, a new toy for her. Anyway, once, when we were about to pull out, that guy, Andrei Belov, defected. Dunno why he did that. Clean files, a loyal Komsomol member, non-Jewish. He ran straight to the American embassy. Smart! He knew that the Swedes might give him a hard time. The Americans were happy. They did everything fast. In three days, he was given an American passport! An order from the admiral came for the ship to stay, and everybody had to remain on board.

"The KGB station chief called me up and said, 'Vanya, you have a girlfriend here. I never objected, even though I should. Never mind that. Belov ought to be brought back. You know Swedish, you have to help.'"

"What could I say? I didn't have anything against the poor bastard. But I had no choice. I went to Ingrid and asked for her help. We needed a car, and a couple of things, you know. She agreed. It was an adventure, and she was always bored. I took two guys with me. We ambushed him, dragged him into Ingrid's car. The KGB chief on board took away his American passport. I will never forget Andrei's eyes. Well, if you want to keep going abroad, you have to do what you are told . . ."

Everybody is silent. I can almost hear the narrator's eyes moving in his eye sockets as he's studying the listeners' reaction. Apparently satisfied with the results of the examination, he pours everybody a half-cup and about one-fourth for the pregnant woman.

"That's too much," she says, giving each man a long flirtatious smile, and pours half of her cup into her husband's. She holds the cup with only four fingers. She's as well endowed as any of Titian's models. She holds her pinky away from the other fingers, another flirtatious device.

"*Nazdorovie!*"

"Cheers!"

The two men bang their cups against one another's, spilling some vodka on the table, and empty the rest in a single gulp. I take a sip and nearly gag. The cup shakes violently in my outstretched hand. The Lieutenant hits me on the back with the palm of his hand and laughs.

"You ain't a *slabak*, brother, are you?"

You don't want to be called a wimp anywhere. But especially not in Russia. Especially not in a car compartment full of strangers and with a nice-looking woman gazing at you appraisingly. I make one giant gulp and empty the cup.

"That's ma boy," the Lieutenant says in a wooden voice reminiscent of his suitcase, and begins to pour more.

"I pass," the woman says. She takes out two boiled eggs, peels them expertly, making not a single nick on their smooth white surface, cuts each in half on an embroidered cloth napkin, salts them liberally, and distributes the pieces among the company.

Her moves are full of ungraceful sexual quality, reminding me that the word "egg" is the Russian slang equivalent of English "nuts."

"I pass, too," I say, risking another *slabak*. The vodka hit my brain so hard that everything around me blurred as if I put on someone else's prescription glasses. My throat burns, and I can't recover my breath completely.

"Come on, man," the Lieutenant says. His cheeks turn flaming-red. "Let's celebrate. People are having a boy. A new man is coming to this world! A soldier. A real man with a real prick, not a fucking pussy."

The husband laughs.

"Watch your language, buddy," the woman says, also smiling, and hits the Lieutenant on his shoulder with her fist. I dread to ask them if they live in Yoshkar-Ola.

Later, the lights are off and everyone but the husband slides under the blankets. The husband leaves for the dining car to see if he can buy some imported strawberry jam. The Lieutenant gives him five rubles for his own jar or two. I close my eyes but the whispers below me force me to open them. From my upper birth, I see that the Lieutenant, now only in his trousers and a T-shirt, sits on the wife's berth and slips his hand under her blanket. I can hear him whispering words like "chocolates, perfume and flowers." She giggles.

I get up and leave the compartment. The cooing couple pays no attention to me. In the aisle, two men shout at each other and flail their hands. I pass by them, my back pressed into the vibrating wall. The train descends deeper and deeper into the depths of the Socialist Camp. The Camp's fence is electrified, its gates are shut. The rain pelts the windows. The train accelerates on its slippery tracks.

Numerology

IT's 1974. I am twenty-four. I wear number 22 over my mostly hairless chest, over a cotton undershirt, checkered flannel shirt and woolen sweater my grandma made for me. My feet are clad in rented ski boots that are too tight for me. As far as I can see, I'm alone in the fir forest, struggling on a path beaten by people who are faster and more experienced than I am. Though I took ski lessons in college and got a C, I still can't compete with the natives. I'm Mari Republic's worst ski racer.

The winner gets a free round-trip rail ticket to Moscow, an overnight ride away. I wish. My only goal is not to be the last one at the finish line. The last skier to cross the line gets his picture taken for the factory's newspaper *Pharmaceuticals to the Motherland* under the caption "a disgrace to our people."

I try to divert myself by trying to crack the significance of the number 22. Maybe it's supposed to depict two skiers sliding downhill one behind another?

Ahead of me, a bunch of my fellow skiers congregate under a snow-covered fir tree. They pass a half-liter bottle around. They drink and then they bend over, pick up a glove-full of powdery snow and eat it.

I stop by them, trying to catch my breath. My fur hat is probably as ugly as theirs.

"You want some?" Nikolai asks. He's an ethnic Mari, a native. His ancestors shot squirrels right in the eye so as not to spoil their skin, and before that, they rode with Genghis Khan on his quest to conquer Russia. Nikolai's frozen breath makes his mustache solid and his yellowish skin snow-white. He works in the lab next to my office. I complain to him every day that I hate it here, that I want to go back to Moscow, and that I'm chained to this place by the law that requires college graduates to work where they are most needed. He listens, interrupting me only with occasional swears directed toward the authorities and the stupid regulations.

Nikolai's family, his wife Zina and their three-year-old daughter Tatiana, lives in the apartment building right next to the plant, in a two-room flat. When the ugly yellow smoke rises from the plant's stacks, his building gets the first whiff of the poison. Zina says it's OK. She says that their windows face the other way, so the neighbors inhale it all in before it gets to them. She works at the same lab as her husband, in quality control. She's quality merchandise herself. Big-busted and friendly. She tells me she's bored, too.

When we danced at the New Year party at the plant's club, she pressed herself into me as if I could shield her from smoke. Afterwards, we went to the lab. She unlocked the door with her key. It was dark inside and it smelled of acetone and some kind of acid. Zina's scent was stronger. When we were done, I apologized to Annie under my breath.

"What is it?" I ask Nikolai now. "Rat poison?"

"Pure alcohol. Two hundred proof. We've got a 100-liter container in the lab."

Ah! Now, I know the secret behind their speed. I drink the liquid from the bottle. It's beyond firewater. It's an atomic explosion in my mouth, throat, and stomach. I cough and belch a mushroom cloud. I rush to swallow enough snow to cover an Olympic-size ski slope.

"Too strong for you, Muscovite?" Nikolai asks. Everyone laughs.

"Let's go," someone suggests.

"No hurry," Nikolai says. "They drink ahead of us, too."

"I'm going," the same man says. "If I win, I'll go to Lenin's Mausoleum. It's my life dream."

In all my years of studying in Moscow, I've never gone to the Mausoleum but I don't want to hurt his feelings. Had Stalin still been there, I would go. So I may spit at him secretly.

Nikolai throws the bottle in the snow. We take off. In a minute or two, only he and I remain. I'm somehow ahead of him.

"Zina's got soft tits, right?" he bellows at the top of his lungs.

Does he know something or is he just probing me, driven by jealousy-enhanced intuition? Whatever it is, I may be in mortal danger. I can't chance it.

We approach a sharp, downward slope. I take my ski polls under my arms and bend like a number 2. It's faster to go down this way. If I try hard, I might make it to the finish line before him. I can't be a disgrace to my people. It would be a mortal mistake.

The Wall Newspaper

It's 1975. I am twenty-five. Today, I'm Martin Luther. I'm nailing my thesis to the church door, which means I'm attaching the plant's newspaper with pushpins to the wall. I'm performing this rebellious act next to the office of my arch-nemesis. He's not the Pope, but the Party boss. This is not Wittenberg, but Yoshkar-Ola, a God-forsaken city 862 kilometers to the east of Moscow. It's still a historical moment, a great revolt nevertheless. Instead of "Hell, purgatory, and heaven," my editorial says, "The plant's cafeteria differs from a pigsty only because it's more expensive."

Normally, people around here fear the Party boss as much as they do the plant director, though the boss is one hierarchal step below. While the latter can make your life hell, the former can make it purgatory. For example, the boss can be instrumental in denying you a government-issued apartment. I don't care about any apartments, and I'm already in purgatory. I want to leave this city of my exile and return to the city of my birth. I want to be close to my parents and my brother. I want to be two thousand kilometers closer to Annie.

The Party boss comes out of his office, reads my editorial and checks out my illustrator Olya's drawings. The boss' hair and the matching tie are shit-brown. Normally, he has to approve the entire issue before it goes up. But that's part of my reformation.

He turns to me and says, "You can lose your job because of that."

"That's the whole point, boss."

"Ah, then you admit that it has nothing to do with the cafeteria? You just want to circumvent the law, right? You want us to get so sick of you that we let you go? I see right through you, kid. The country paid for your college education. The country wants you to work here. So you will work here for as long as law requires it. Two more years, kid. Like it or not."

"No, sir. It has nothing to do with the law. The cafeteria food stinks, and you know this."

He stares at me. I stare back. He slithered up to his position partially because they want to promote ethnic Maris, the local minority, and partially because he's so stubborn. I'm also stubborn. We stand on our hind legs and lock our horns for a long time.

The trouble is my so-called "wall newspaper" has a circulation of one. If the boss tears it down, I'm finished. Who will I complain to? Olya and I spent so much time making it.

I say, "The Party teaches us to tell the truth. If someone gets sick again in the cafeteria, it will be an indelible stain on the plant's reputation. On your reputation, comrade."

He drops his gaze and retreats to the safety of his office. I've been in there more than once. He has a black leather chair for himself, two plain chairs for visitors, a gilded-framed Lenin on the wall, and a color TV. There are heavy draperies on the windows, so he could close them to get cozy with the female apartment petitioners or with his secretary Agraphena Agaphonovna, a woman with a substantial derrière. Seeing his retreat, the office workers assemble behind me. They read the editorial and laugh. I guess the churchgoers did the same for Luther.

"The dying are freed by death from all penalties . . . Ha-ha-ha! Martin, buddy, you're so funny!"

At the dorm, in my own private room, I take six eggs that I store between the regular and the storm windows. The eggs are frozen solid. I bought this precious commodity *po blatu*: I was flirting with the grocery store clerk. I take them to the communal kitchen, grease the skillet with a tablespoon of sunflower oil, crack the eggs, and drop them into the skillet. For a while, they stand there like six miniature stone columns that support the heavy kitchen air. I return to my room the size of a monk's cell and feast like an abbot.

The next day, I go to the cafeteria for lunch. I order a meat patty, mashed potatoes and compote. They are made from wood dust, roadkill, industrial glue and tree leaves in a sugary syrup. That's what my editorial says. After a brief hesitation, I also order soup, which is made of last year's beans, chicken feed and polluted water from the Volga River.

I sit next to Olya, who is also the plant's junior bookkeeper, 3rd Class. She has the same order because they have nothing else on the menu. In the newspaper, she drew a pig that is pushing away a plate. The drawing has a caption, "Even a pig refuses this refuse." She came up with the caption on her own.

"Did he tear it down?" she asks. "You know he's not eating here?"

I instructed her to tell the boss that she did everything I told her, and that she is not responsible for anything. In truth, I wish she would do everything that I told her, but she has a fiancé.

"He wouldn't dare," I say.

She lays her hand on top of mine. If she were a sixteenth-century nun, she would say, *"Impetum inimicorum ne timueritis."* If she were the nineteenth-century Turgenev damsel, she would say the same thing but in Russian, "You should not fear the attack of enemies." But now she says, "Don't you mind a jerk like him."

"It's no use," I say. "I need to go to Moscow to petition for my release in person."

She sighs. She is a native Yoshkar-Ola-er, and has no place to go. "Are you sure you can find a job back home?"

I nod. I'm not sure. Here, I'm an engineer, 2nd Class. Back home, I would start as the 3rd Class at best. But I just can't stand this anymore.

We eat. Two weeks ago, I vomited after a meal like this. So did Olya. The Party boss says we have weak stomachs. Not for fighting, though.

"Maybe you should write an article for the *Mari Pravda*?" Olya says.

That's an idea. *Mari Pravda* is a real newspaper. If they publish my article, the plant's kingpins will have no choice but to send me packing.

"Good idea. Care to help?"

"Sure," she says. After work, we come to the library where we usually put the newspaper together. It's locked. No signs are posted. Very strange.

"It's a conspiracy," Olya says. "They don't want us to do it."

"Let's go to the dorm," I say. "They have a community room."

Outside, the snow crunches underfoot. Olya covers her face with a scarf. She lost all her womanly shape under the layers. My breath forms ice on my mustache. Back home, in Moldova, the snow doesn't stay long, and the spring comes quickly. Back home, I would be with my parents and my brother. I miss them. Well, I wouldn't see Volodya anyway. He travels all over the country, installing control equipment at chemical plants. But my parents are still there, teaching. And my grandparents are still alive. We could have family dinners at night and talk about everything.

I get closer to Olya to protect her against the wind. Our mittened hands meet.

It turns out they are holding a chess tournament in the community room. I sigh.

"But you have your own room, don't you?" Olya asks.

I blush. My room is too sinful for a bride.

I unlock the door and let her in. We take off our heavy coats. She sits in the room's only chair, and I sit on the bed. It's not that cold here. I'm probably getting to be a real Yoshkar-Ola-er. I give Olya a pen and paper, and we begin to write. In the middle of the first sentence, our naked hands touch, and we begin to kiss. Soon, we dispose of all the layers, and slide under the blankets. But then my stomach churns loudly. Olya disengages from me. Her small breasts are milky in the moonlight. I'm torn. It's worse than getting a laxative and a sleeping pill at the same time.

"I'm not feeling well," she says, her hand on her flat stomach. I hear the loud murmur of her peristalsis. "Where is your bathroom?"

We are getting dressed in a hurry, as if we are a monk and nun caught in a lewd act by a band of outraged Protestants led by Martin Luther himself. Tomorrow, I will grab the Party boss by his bull's neck and force-feed him the cafeteria hamburger, mashed potatoes, soup and compote.

One teaspoon at a time.

The Art of Spelling

It's 1976. I am twenty-six. I am back at my home city. Dr. Rabinovitz asks me to open my mouth wide and say, *a-a-a*. Three As in a row.

When I was little, I wondered why doctors favor this letter over all other vowels. Then it dawned on me to come to the mirror and compare the mouth opening with an A to an E, U or even O. Those clever doctors, they knew everything. I will be a doctor, I told myself. But my father said that doctors have to cut up cadavers in medical school.

"What's a cadaver?" I asked. It sounded like a doctor's word. Two As.

"A dead human body."

"Yak," I said and stuck out my tongue. That didn't sound like much fun. I'd rather cut an electrical wire to see why they won't let me touch it.

Now, Dr. Rabinovitz checks my tongue. "I don't see anything," he says. "The tongue looks normal. No fever."

"I have a cough," I say. "*Khe-khe-khe!* Hear that?"

"OK. I'll give you a *bolnichny*," he says. "Stay home for three days."

That's what I wanted. In the Soviet Union, you need a doctor's *bolnichny* to skip work. I give him another *khe-khe*, my best one so far, and smile.

"Do you want to meet a nice girl?" he asks. That's so unfair. Do you ask a cat if she wants tuna fish? Do you ask a CEO if he wants power?

I lower my head and blush. I can blush at will.

"Her name is Carmen," he adds. "She's a medical student."

The other day, my brother told me that most bachelors overrate casual sex. He knows what he's talking about. He's already married to a girl named Sylvia, who could have been like a sister to me had I met her more than a few times. "It's not that sex is not good after marriage," he said. "But now it's linked to procreation, making it much more meaningful. It's a totally different experience. Take it from me."

Now, I take the phone number from Dr. Rabinovitz and pocket it next to a condom.

On the way home, I stop at a phone booth and call Carmen. The following day, we walk among rose bushes in the park, hand-in-hand. I just finished eating the candies I bought for her—she is on a diet. I entertain her with my usual arsenal of trivia and jokes. I'm an indestructible charm machine, smooth and naturally well-oiled.

I say, "When Duke Leopold of Austria went into a battle once, he wore a white shirt with a belt. The shirt turned red from his wounds, except for the white strip under the belt. That's how the Austrian flag was born. As for the Soviet flag, our revolutionary soldiers were probably beltless."

Carmen bats her eyelashes at me and squeezes my hand. Her eyes are the most beautiful light-sensing devices I've ever seen. Blue iris, clearest whites and lush black lashes. Some exotic island country should have a flag with these three colors.

"Did you like to dissect frogs when you were a little girl?" I ask.

She laughs. "Anatomy is my favorite subject."

In the evening, we kiss by her door, and when I fall asleep back at my place, we explore each other's anatomy in a Viennese castle.

"Do you want to go to a birthday party with me?" Carmen says the next day. "I bet you you've never seen so many medical students in one place. Just be careful with Lyuba. She's a man eater."

Funny she should ask.

When we enter a most ordinary apartment in a gray, concrete building, the music assaults me. I shake my head, let go of Carmen's hand and cover my ears. And then I see Her. It seems like everyone else's faces are smeared like in an unfocused photograph, and only Hers is in focus.

I feel as if Duke Leopold has hit me over the head with his mace. I can barely stand. The indestructible machine puffs, smokes and falters. Her eyes. They're not gems like Carmen's. Good-looking brown eyes, but that's just the physical surface. Little devils and little angels shimmy in pairs inside them. They all have the same face. And that face is mine.

I tell myself, "I will marry her, if she lets me." I'm ready to follow Her on my knees until she does. When Russian pilgrims of old used to come to the Holy Land, they would crawl on their knees all the way from the seaport to Jerusalem. Am I less determined? Of course not.

Carmen tugs on my hand. Funny, I forgot all about her. No, it's not funny. It's just fate. Fate can't be funny or serious. Like nature, fate is neutral. It does what has to be done, and it makes no excuses.

How can I describe perfection with imperfect words? How can I put a shape to something ethereal? How can I stop something that is so fleeting? But I've never turned away from an impossible task, and now is not the time to change a life-long habit. So I must take out my quill and prepare to write.

> *Spill my name from your lips.*
> *Let it break into clear beads*
> *before it reaches the floor.*
> *Let it scatter.*
> *Let it be silent.*
> *Don't worry.*
> *Your lips*
> *will shape my name*
> *again,*
> *from the wind,*
> *from the fragrance of milk,*
> *from the smell of honey,*
> *from fragments of words,*
> *and scraps of sounds*
> *lost by birds, by cars, by your cat,*
> *lost in familiar patterns:*
> *of smiling, kissing and teasing.*
> *Spell my name,*
> *let it go.*

I approach Her and ask for a dance. My tongue is tripping over my teeth. She looks up to me and smiles.

"You're so tall," she says. "Uncle, get a birdy." That's a line from a children's poem. She looks childlike, though she's got to be the same age as Carmen, twenty-two. Curls of dark gold dance on her shoulders.

I want to say something witty, but my tongue is still aching from its fall. She touches her finger to my lips. A devil and an angel jump out of her eyes, and rub my ears red. My indestructible machine comes to life again, but, instead of the charm offense, it pours out simple, unadorned words that have nothing to do with poetry.

On the way home, I'm thinking of Annie. Am I betraying her? Lyuba is like Annie when she was fourteen, but a bit taller, and her hair is of a lighter color. The rest is the same. Same big eyes, same Mona Lisa smile. It's like *The Comedy of Errors*, except that it's tragic.

I can't help myself. If I am a betrayer, a monster, an oath breaker, so be it.

Five months later, Lyuba and I are married in a civil ceremony. Lyuba means "love" in Russian. The marriage official wears a gold-plated chain on her plump chest. Her lipstick is smeared. Perhaps she's supposed to kiss the groom. A few links lost their gold, and we can see the underlying base metal. We fight hard to suppress giggles. Our giggles are so contagious that her lips begin to tremble as well.

"You may kiss the bride," she says. I kiss my wife, and smear her lipstick.

The official doesn't kiss me, and I consider tipping for this.

The reception takes place in the restaurant called Intourist, which literally means "for foreign tourists." I take this as an omen. We will leave the country one day.

Now, we live alone in our own apartment, a rarity for a young Soviet couple. There is a balcony covered by vines, and sometimes we venture there to feel the warmth of the night on our bare skin.

When I get used to my wife, I can see that she is a sapphire while Annie is a diamond. Which stone is more precious? I'm not a gem connoisseur. I love my wife, and this is love at first sight, but I still long for Annie. She's my second cousin after all. So it's a mixture of brotherly and physical love. On the other hand, it's perfectly legit. Even my Volodya would agree, but I don't ask him. He's too busy for me.

Anyway, Annie is just an abstraction, as unattainable as a girl from the dark side of the moon. I will never be able even to touch her. Comparing these two women is a mindless game.

My wife and I go to Leningrad for the honeymoon. We stay in my wife's distant relatives' apartment, and sleep in a room full of clocks.

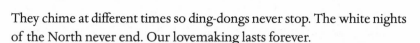

They chime at different times so ding-dongs never stop. The white nights of the North never end. Our lovemaking lasts forever.

We come back, unpack, have supper, and get ready for bed. The glass in the window rattles later that evening.

"Some stupid kids are knocking," I say. An annoying dimwit youngster lives upstairs from us. His parents lock him up on the balcony, and he climbs up and down the waterspout. At night, he hoots like an owl.

"It's an earthquake," my wife says. I grin. It's my first earthquake. The word sounds very romantic, like climbing up the Himalayans or diving into Niagara Falls.

We run outside. A few dimwit youngsters hoot, but the rest of the sidewalk is full of dazed citizens who apparently find nothing funny or romantic in the situation. My wife is barefooted. I give her my slippers and come back for her coat. Now, the walls are shaking, too. It's dark and it smells of airborne dust and burning insulation. I come out with her coat just before the ceiling in the hallway falls. No one knows how many people die this night or how many buildings collapse. If someone keeps count, they are not telling us. We are lucky. We are not even scratched, and our apartment is still livable.

We play Scrabble every weekend. My wife wins four games out of five. I tell her that I get bad letters all the time, but she doesn't laugh. She tells me to get good letters. Playing Scrabble comes naturally to her, like a baby's cry when she's hungry. We played chess at first as well, but I won every time. We love each other, and our love gets stronger with every game of Scrabble. Let the best speller win.

Country Roads

It's 1978. I am twenty-eight. If I'm late today, I'm court-martialed.

The bus station building is just a concrete frame, rough, windowless, completely open on one side, with a long wooden bench along the back wall. Dirty words, mostly in Russian, are carved into the wood of the bench, painted on the walls, and penciled across cheerful propaganda slogans. Heat pours inside, wave after wave unresisted. A smell of urine and rotten garbage hangs in the air. A Moldovian woman in a short-sleeved pink dress with big patches of sweat under her arms sells tickets. A silver coin on a thin brass chain nests comfortably between her plump breasts.

I approach her, staring at beads of sweat on her round peasant face, at her tanned, generously exposed neck. I open my mouth, then close it, and return to the bench. I'm hopelessly and helplessly lost. I'm considering either committing suicide or taking off my army boots and hiding in the bushes until the end of time.

A motorcycle comes to a screeching halt in a cloud of dust and blue nauseous smoke next to the station. The biker is a short, unassuming man in his fifties, with a skin so tanned that he looks like an Arab. He wears a dirty white undershirt, brown baggy pants and plastic sandals on his bare feet. *"Unde duc?"* he asks me in Moldovan.

I've hated this language ever since I was forced to study it in school. It's not Slavic-based, so it sounds totally alien. We, Russian-speakers, mocked the Moldovian teacher, a retired army veteran, until the man screamed and hammered the table with his fist. Then we stopped for a short while, only to repeat the whole ordeal later. We called him a *tsaran*, a peasant, the name reserved for all Moldovan-speaking Moldovians, regardless of their occupation and intellectual abilities.

"Going to my base," I reply to the biker in Russian now.

"Aha," says the biker. He thinks for a moment, and says in Russian, with an unexpectedly mild accent, "Where is your base?"

"I don't know. I'm lost."

"Okay," says the biker, and spits on the ground. "There will be no more buses today," he says.

"I've got to get to my base tonight," I say. "If I don't, they'll court-martial me."

"Aha," the biker says and sits down next to me. Besides sweat, he smells of gasoline, onions and sour wine.

"I'm on leave," I say. "They brought us to the base at night. They never told us its location. It's supposed to be a secret. Yesterday they gave me a ride to Kishinev, on an Army bus, also at night. I've got to get back. But I don't know my way. I thought it's some place around this village. I took a bus to here, but now I'm stuck. I don't know what to do. I fell through the cracks. It probably looks funny, but it's a terrible mess."

"Aha," the biker says. He pulls out a cigarette from behind his ear, puts it in his mouth, but does not light it. "I can give you a ride to Kishinev," he says.

"I need to get to my base," I say.

"You're a lieutenant," the biker says. "How come you don't know your way?"

"I'm a reserve officer. I've never been in this area before. And they don't give us maps. I thought I'd find it somehow. Shit."

"Aha," the biker says. He thinks for a while, staring at the fringe on the bottom of his too-short pants. "I know two bases around here. Does yours have just tents or are there real brick barracks there?"

"Tents," I say. My heart pounds inside my chest as if it wants to jump out and shout, "Help me!"

"Both bases I know have tents," the biker says.

"Are you pulling my leg?" I say.

"What leg?" the biker says. "They both have tents. If you want to, we could try both."

I sit behind the biker, holding on tight to a hot chrome bar. My knuckles turn white. My body sweats, itches and aches in very unlikely places. I feel on the higher level of consciousness like a French aristocrat about to be guillotined, and on the lower, down-to-earth level, like a fish about to be gutted. Dust sticks to the wet stains on my uniform, accumulating layer upon layer. I quit wiping off my face ages ago.

Earlier that morning my wife and I kissed on the floor of our one-bedroom apartment while our six-month-old daughter crawled over us acting as a chastity belt. I was already dressed in my generously-wrinkled khaki uniform and high black boots of the roughest artificial leather imaginable. Instead of socks, I wore *portyanki*, pieces of cloth wrapped around my feet to prevent blisters. My daughter pulled on my khaki epaulet adorned with two tiny yellow stars.

"I could write you a *bolnichny*," my wife said again. A *"bolnichny"* is a doctor's note.

"I told you, they won't believe me," I said. "Sick or not sick, I have to be back tonight. It's my turn to be the regiment's duty officer. Anyway, only Moldovians write *bolnichnys*."

"I don't know about you, but I'm really sick," my wife said. "I'm sick of your war games."

"You're acting as if I had a choice," I said.

Actually, I did have a choice. My friend had told me about one clever draft-avoiding technique.

"They call extra people just in case," he had explained. "So if you have enough guts not to show up in the first place, they might have a sufficient number of heads and leave you alone."

I don't have enough guts to cheat.

"Here's the camp," the biker says now. "Is it yours?"

He stops his machine on the top of the hill, pointing to khaki tents below lined up like a bunch of ugly cousins. A horde of vehicles of all sizes is parked nearby. The setting sun blazes fiercely in their windshields.

"I don't think so," I say slowly. I'm not sure of anything anymore. My mind seems bleached and erased.

"Okay, that leaves us only one choice," the biker says.

We drive without saying a word. The wind throws buckets of dust in our faces. Then a muffled clap of thunder hits my ears. A great inhuman force pulls the bar from my hands and throws me into the air. I hover there for what seems to be a long, long time, but instead of seeing my life pass before me, as I am supposed to do according to everything I've read, I just think pure and virgin nothingness.

I finally land, properly, thanks to my karate reflexes. I feel almost no pain. The biker lies on his face on the other side of the dirt road. The overturned bike's wheels are still rotating. I inch my way toward my fallen comrade. "Are you okay?" I ask in a coarse voice. Something warm and moist is on my own forehead, but I'm afraid to touch it. There is almost no pain.

What if he's dead? Do I have to bury him?

As if worrying about my anxiety, the biker turns on his back and then sits up. "The damn tire blew up," he says, turning off the ignition. "Are you OK?"

"Yes."

"Then help me. I need to get the bike to that tree."

We drag the lifeless thing for about fifty meters. Then the biker produces a chain and a lock from a hidden compartment inside the bike. "Let's go," he says when he's done chaining the bike.

"Where to?"

"To the second camp, where else?"

We walk for a while before I dare to ask, "How far is that?"

"Not far."

The young night has already arrived. Illustrious stars shine like tsar's jewels, too bright and gaudy to dress up the simple country skies. The moon looks at home, however, with its broad and smiling peasant's face. The dirt road, surrounded on both sides by immense vineyards, just goes on, and on, and on. Occasional lights from the distant houses look unrealistically inviting. Dogs bark somewhere. I don't dare to check the time. I hope my watch is broken from the impact of the crash. Perhaps I can use the accident as a feeble excuse for my lateness.

"What's your name?" I ask the biker after a while.

"Nicolae."

Nicolae walks with a slight stoop, even though he is far from being tall. But he moves fast, in a relaxed, athletic manner. My *portyankis* come loose, and my feet are rubbing against the harsh insides of my boots.

"Wait," I say, and sit down right in the middle of the dirt road. I pull off my boots. My feet stink beyond the limits of human endurance. My *portyankis* are a tangled mess. I re-wrap them around my feet, and am about to begin the painful process of putting the boots back on when Nicolae stops me.

"Let me show you," he says, sitting down next to me, and wrapping the cloth in a couple of swift and accurate moves. His nose wrinkles at the smell.

Then we walk some more, and we see the lights.

"Puzheni," Nicolae says. "The base is very close to here."

We walk down the village's empty street, along the row of accurate little houses, each half-hidden behind a wooden fence. Not a single human soul greets us, only the dogs bark viciously from behind the fences, and a stray black cat runs across the road right in front of our feet. We make it all the way through the village, until the houses begin to get sparse and the lights become almost nonexistent. Then we see two men in our path. One of them holds an empty bottle in his hand, by the neck, as if he wants to throw it away and quit drinking forever.

"*Buna sara*, good evening," Nicolae greets the men. His voice sounds steady. They don't answer, just move a little closer. A wine aroma, thick and sour, envelopes us.

"Got a smoke?" the man with the bottle asks me in Russian. His accent is thick.

"I don't smoke," I answer. Nicolae steps ahead and says something in Moldovan that I don't understand.

"Fuck you," the man with the bottle says. The other one, without saying a word, smashes his fists against Nicolae's face. Nicolae's head jerks back, but he remains on his feet. I step towards the man who hit Nicolae and, forgetting all the karate lessons, smash my booted feet into the man's leg right below the knee.

The man collapses on the ground like a fallen tree. The other one, shouting something in Moldovan, makes wild clumsy motions with his feet and hands. He drops the bottle and hardly keeps his balance.

I swing my right hand at him, and the man turns around and flees. He falls, gets up, and runs again. The first one still lies on the ground, clutching his foot and shouting obscenities in both languages.

"Let's go," Nicolae says, gently pulling me by the sleeve away from the fallen man. My teeth are chattering even though the night is hot. "Sons of bitches," I say.

We walk some more, silently. The night is full with aromas of summer earth. Bugs sing in the international language of love and brotherhood.

"Drunken sons of bitches," I say again. "They should be exterminated, damn drunkards. They should have their balls cut off. They should be shot. They should be hanged. They should . . ."

Nicolae is silent.

"Does it hurt?" I ask.

"No."

"What do you do for a living?" I say about a hundred meters later.

"I'm a *kolhosnik*."

"A farmer, huh? And I'm an engineer. Do you have kids?"

"Got three."

"I have one. A girl. She's the best girl there is."

We walk some more. A dull glow appears behind the horizon.

"You know," I say, "I never had a Moldovian friend before."

"I knew that," Nicolae says.

"How did you know?"

"I know. I saw you."

"I'm not prejudiced. By the way, my roots are here. My ancestors lived here ever since the Turkish War. That's almost two hundred years. Impressive, huh?"

"Here we are," Nicolae says.

In a valley below, an entity, a giant beast rumbles, and stinks, and shakes the earth. The beast stares at us with scores of moving, blazing eyes, its tentacles waving frantically, its body shuddering.

"Is this your camp?" Nicolae asks.

"I don't know. Let's get closer and check."

"I can't get closer. Civilians are not supposed to."

"Then wait for me, please. I'll be right back."

"I'll wait," he said. "I have time."

I run down to the gates of the compound. A sentry armed with an AK-47 stops me.

"Is it you, Ivanov?" I ask.

"Aye, sir," the man answers, letting me through. I run toward the guard's tent. Nobody is there but a small reddish dog that licks my boots delightfully. I run to the officer's tent, followed by the dog. Inside the great tent, under a dim bare bulb hanging from a post, four men are playing cards on beds covered with rough woolen blankets.

"Look who's here," said one of them. "And we thought that you deserted."

And they all laugh.

"C'mon guys, what's happened?" I say. "Were they looking for me?"

"Sure they were. They even called the military police. With dogs."

"Dogs?"

"Oh yeah, dogs. Here's one of them," and the man points toward the small reddish creature that cringes before us on the dirt floor. My feet give out, and I sit, almost fall down, on the bed.

"Relax, buddy," another man says. "Karpenko took your place. Nobody cared. Nobody has even noticed."

"Are you sure?"

"Of course I am," the same man says. "Just don't forget you owe him. A bottle of nice wine would do, he said."

"You play poker?" the first man says. "Care to join us?"

I take some cards in my shaky hands. My head is empty, like the wine bottles that litter the tent.

Above us, on the top of the hill, Nicolae lights a cigarette, and sends a puff of smoke toward the deep skies of his homeland. He's waiting. He's patient. He has all the time in the world.

The Keepers of Karma

It's 1979. I am twenty-nine. I am a hereditary immigrant. My grand-parents immigrated twice without moving out of their house. They had no choice. Russia, Romania and the Soviet Union arranged the process for them by moving the borders back and forth. My parents immigrated once in the same manner. Then Stalin came, and sent them into internal exile.

When I was little, I waded into the Black Sea until the water reached my cute belly button. I asked my father, "What's on the other side?"

"Bulgaria," he said. That sounded dry, like an arid bagel.

"And after that?"

"Western Europe."

I knew what a Western was—a movie where they ride horses and fight Indians.

"And after that?"

"The Atlantic Ocean."

"And behind the ocean?"

"America."

I knew Americans wore top hats, smoked cigars, exploited workers and wanted to bomb everybody, especially my Motherland. But I didn't know they were that far.

"What is closer, America or the moon?"

"Spanking," my dad said with his usual half-smile. "That's the closest thing to you." He thought for a second and added, "Violence determines conciseness."

I didn't know he was making a Russian language pun on the Marxist maxim "Environment determines conciseness."

Now, on this summer day in 1979, my parents are leaving for America and so will I. Not only because I love them, but because I can't breath the Soviet air any longer. But the government wants me to dance on a hot skillet first.

I go to my company's head office and announce myself. The secretary's dark eyes, heavily made up, remind me of an Egyptian temple priestess who used to offer free love to pilgrims. Any second now, she will tear off her flower-patterned summer dress and lie down on the table, beckoning me impatiently with her left hand, while still typing with the right. I will decline, of course. I'm married.

Once, a story around the company goes, the secretary poured insecticide into her electric typewriter to kill a roach, causing a small fire. We call her Vesta.

Instead of undressing, Vesta continues to pound away at the fixed typewriter. Her black-rimmed eyes stare at me as if I am a roach. She smells of some artificial flower, a product of a Soviet industrial design. I doubt any real priestess's eyes would be that smudged. They would fire her for that.

"I'm here to see Mr. Ivanenko," I say meekly.

"If it's about getting an apartment," Vesta says, looking at the crown of my head, "you have to see Mr. Petrov first."

"It's not about the apartment."

"Sit," Vesta says. Perhaps someone, somewhere, sometime, will sound more unfriendly than her.

I lower myself into a vinyl chair, worn out by the rumps of previous generations of petitioners. My thoughts drift from guessing what's under her summer dress and from what I would have done to her if I weren't married, to whether or not Mr. Ivanenko will shake my hand.

Vesta gets up and disappears behind the leather-encased door. I examine my fingernails. I examine the tips of my worn shoes. I examine the linoleum of the floor, freshly replaced near the desk, where it was scorched by fire.

I hear muted sounds from behind the door but can't make out the words. Does Vesta perform some unspeakable sexual rites on Mr. Ivanenko? Does she dance naked around a three-legged brazier full of burning coals? Does Mr. Ivanenko accompany her on a drum?

Vesta emerges. Her shoulders are slumped. Now she smells of coal. "You may come in," she says.

Behind the door, Mr. Ivanenko is mounted on a tall-backed chair, a pen in his hand like a scepter. There is no brazier or drum. Mr. Ivanenko looks me in the eyes. "Yes?" he says.

Should I bow or say hello? I think. I clear my throat. "Good day, Mr. Ivanenko."

"Yes?" he repeats. The note of impatience reverberates in his voice.

"I need your sign-off on my application to leave the country," I say.

He moves his lips but no sound comes out. His gaze pushes heavily on my shoulders. "You would have to resign from the company first, if you want me to sign-off," he says. "We can't keep traitors to the Fatherland employed here."

When I get home, I show the sign-off paper to Lyuba. She nods. She doesn't want to go to America, but the Afghan war is on. Last week, she burned my draft summons. Luckily, they just dropped it off at the mailbox instead of forcing me to sign for it. She didn't tell me. She is the bravest woman I've ever known. If the secretary is Vesta, then my wife is Athena.

"What are we going to eat?" she says. Her tears are all dried up now. Even powerful goddesses cry sometimes. They had fired her when she received her sign-off. "What will I feed Mila?"

"I'll find another job," I say.

My next sign-off is the military commissariat. That will be a tough one.

Before going to bed, I read an underground pamphlet about Stalin. I know a thing or two about him. He sent my grandparents to Siberia to chop wood.

I remember talking to my granddad about that. I was seven.

"What did you do," I asked. "Try to kill Stalin?"

"No, I owned a wine bar. No employees. Just me and Grandma."

"You were a capitalist?"

"Well, it was under the Romanians. It was legal to own a store then."

It was legal to be a capitalist swine? I didn't want to press the issue because I loved him.

The author of the pamphlet spent twenty years in the Gulag. Now, he writes about the Keepers of Karma who maintain the order in this world. When Stalin died, the keepers tried to drag his soul to Hell. The soul was very powerful. It resisted. It knocked out the keepers one by one. It was just like the scene I'd observed once when a big drunkard fought a bunch of cops.

My wife turns off the lights, so I don't have a chance to find out who won, Stalin or the keepers.

The next day, I sit at the bench in the commissariat. The bench is bolted to the floor, to protect it from the thieving imperialist spies. The sergeant behind the desk reads a newspaper. On a poster above him, a Russian soldier bayonets his American counterpart, while a capitalist swine in a top hat watches with horror. The phone buzzes. The sergeant listens to the voice on the other end, and then barks to me, "You next!"

I knock at the door and enter the office. To my horror, the major who stands by the window looks like Stalin. Same mass of hair combed over the low forehead. Same bushy mustache. Same penetrating, pig eyes. Even the pipe is the same.

"Why didn't you come when we summoned you, Lieutenant?" Stalin asks. "Do you know that we can jail you for that?"

"I didn't get any summons," I say honestly. Once I applied to leave, it was too late to give the summons to me. The government invents stupid rules, but this time they work in my favor.

"They boy who delivers the summons should be shot," Stalin says. "The lazy bastard didn't serve it to you right!"

I disagree, but I keep my mouth shut. Everybody else who disagreed with Stalin is dead. You can't argue with statistics.

"Why are you leaving the country?" He puffs smoke. He needs to lose some weight. Isn't he afraid of cancer?

"I want to join my parents," I offer the well-rehearsed phrase. Technically, they don't have that much power over me. I'm only a reservist, though they did confer the rank of a lieutenant on me back in college. I don't think that they would bother with technicalities, though. This guy in front of me never did.

"You're a traitor to the Fatherland," he says.

I shift my weight from one foot to the other. It looks like the Keepers of Karma have not succeeded after all.

"Do you know what they do to people like you in jail, boy?" he asks, pointing his pipe at me as if it is a Makarov pistol. "Answer me!"

I snap to attention. "Can't know that, sir!"

He comes close and puffs a cloud of smoke at me. I resist the need to cough.

"I can personally shoot you on the spot," he says. "I'll tell them that you attacked me."

Before you do that, Joseph, I'll ram your pipe down your throat, I think.

He reads my eyes and steps back. "Where is your fucking sign-off?"

I give him the paper. He signs it and gives it back to me. "Get the fuck out of here."

I leave. I feel like he blew acrid smoke into my very soul. But I've heard that they are hiring workers in a glass factory. You need to walk on top of a furnace in a pair of boots with heels three inches thick so your feet won't get burned. So what? They pay well. The government will let me leave the country in a year or two. I am sure of that. So, the hell with him. He only looks like Stalin, anyway. Really, Stalin is long dead, and the Keepers of Karma took care of him.

Once outside, I open the paper and read his signature. My heart quits beating. My blood stops flowing. My breathing halts. He did sign *Stalin*. He rendered the sign-off invalid. I'm doomed.

I see two men approaching me. The Keepers of Karma? But I'm not dead yet. No, it's the cops sent by Stalin. Two cops, jackbooted, in peaked caps, and wrinkled uniforms. They smell of raw earth as if they have spent a long time sleeping on bunk beds in some God-forsaken underground barrack.

I assume a karate stand. I'll fight them. I'll show them what a man who values his freedom can do. Yet they pass by me as if I don't even exist.

When my hands stop shaking, I check the signature again. It's not *Stalin*. It's *Stolin*. Close, but different. *Stolin* is a good, old Russian name, not sputtered by blood. While *Stalin* is death and slavery, *Stolin* is life and freedom. I can go now. We can go.

Hunger

It's still 1979. I am still twenty-nine. While waiting for an exit visa, my family is starving. Even semi-Americans have to eat, and future prosperity won't feed us now. That's one of the negative things about socialism: humans are slaves of their stomachs. I'm sure things are different in America because there slavery has long been abandoned.

I'm always hungry, ever since I remember myself. I couldn't figure out why my parents had very little to eat. I thought that something was wrong with me and my appetite. I'm trying to restrain myself now, but I often fail.

I spend all my time looking for a new job, but no one wants to hire a traitor to the Fatherland. Everyone turns me away as soon as they find out who I am. Everyone except for the glass factory manager.

He offers me a beaten-up wooden chair in his office. Besides a Brezhnev, the wall holds a photograph of the manager standing by a heap of bottles that are taller than he. In it he smiles. If I were him I wouldn't have smiled. I would've been afraid that the heap would collapse and bury me.

The office's only window faces a smoke stack that belches something dark-brown with occasional splashes of bright red. The manager barely checks my papers. His face is the shape and color of a fresh tomato.

"People don't realize how important this business is," he says. "All bottles are made of glass, right? What do people drink their vodka from? Right, from bottles! What would society do without us? Right, it would fall apart."

When he gets up, he seems taller than me until I realize that the soles of his boots are three inches thick.

I nod. I agree with his assessment. People do drink vodka from bottles.

"No one wants to work here," he says. "They think it's too damn hot. Are you afraid of the heat?"

"No," I say. "I'm afraid of the cold. I hate sneezing. Sneezing makes me want to cough, and coughing is bad for you."

"You're funny," he says. "I like you. Have you installed control devices before?"

I studied that in college, four years ago. It's a tedious job. You have to crawl into tight spaces, and your joints ache at the end of the day.

"Sure," I say. "Installing control devices is my favorite pastime. I can do it with my eyes closed and with one hand tied behind my back."

"Perfect. You're hired as an electro-mechanic. We'll pay you 120 rubles a month. Since you have a degree, you'll be the shift supervisor in six months if you do a good job. Deal?"

Electro-mechanic is a mere technician, but 120 rubles is as much as I was making at my previous, engineering job. Lyuba, Mila and I are saved from starvation by the man in funny boots with the face of a vegetable. When I'll tell this to my future American friends, they will die laughing.

"Deal," I say.

We shake hands. He wears gloves, and I wonder if his hands are the same color and consistency as his face is.

I don't tell my wife about the smoke stack, only about 120 rubles. She has other things to worry about. Like standing in line at the grocery store.

The following day, I walk to work to save five kopecks for the bus fare. I carry my engineering briefcase with me, which contains, instead of blueprints, two bologna sandwiches my wife made for me. I walk along the rail tracks and try to out-whistle the trains. Then I sing an aria from *Aida*. Then I read aloud a new haiku I just concocted:

> *All hands clap; delight*
> *reigns like an Eastern king*
> *untroubled by flies.*

I meet my coworkers. Petruha, the day shift supervisor, is several inches taller than me and his hands are as long as orangutan's paws. He says that he's a semi-retired thief. Ionel, his right-hand man, looks like an obedient dog, but he nods all the time instead of wiggling his tail. Victor, his left-hand man, introduces himself as a "free spirit." That's the whole brigade. An ape and his two hands. I will be his tail, until I learn the ropes.

"Why are you here?" Victor asks. I tell him.

"Ah, a traitor," he says casually. "It's OK. We all are pariahs here. A normal man wouldn't work in this place."

Petruha gives me worn overalls and boots with three-inch soles. There is a hole with burned edges in the overalls' chest.

"It was Sasha's," Petruha says. "The melting glass escaped from the furnace and killed him. You should have heard how he cried before he died. Wait a minute; your name is Sasha, too. How funny."

"Alex," I say. "My name is Alex."

"Don't scare the man," Victor says. "The poor slob's name was Grisha."

Petruha leads me to the furnace. "We lose the signal from a thermo-couple," he says. "It's an intermittent problem. I think the cable has a short. Find where the short is, and splice the cable." He points to a crawl space under the furnace. "Understand?"

The heat from the furnace scorches my face from ten yards away. It's a small sun. The planet Mercury, at least. I need a thermal suit, which they don't have, naturally.

"Sure," I say. "Nothing to it."

I douse my overalls with water, open the trap door and climb inside. A naked bulb hanging on a wire barely illuminates this place. Needles tremble inside dimly lit scales. Steam hisses, escaping from a pipe. Now, Biblical Enoch was taken alive to heaven. As for me, I willingly go to hell for 120 rubles. Any sinner should come to this place to get an idea what's in store for him. This is not the Nordic idea of hell, which is supposed to be cold, but the hot, Middle Eastern one.

I feel the cable with my gloved hand. It's frail, and it should be in such an environment. I follow along, and find the place where it's completely stripped of insulation. The exposed strands of wire are covered with rust.

I take a few gulps from my water bottle. I turn off the switch and splice the cable. I'm wetter than a seal that just emerged from the ocean, and my face probably looks like a peeled tomato, but I'm done. Nothing to it.

I turn around and find the trap door locked. I push, but it doesn't budge. I shout and bang at the door with the handle of the splicing knife. Nothing. I'm trapped. I forgot what makes the idea of hell so ingeniously clever. It's not just torture. It's torture that lasts forever, and there is no escape. Even when you get an American visa.

I take a few more sips of water and splash some on my face. They don't die in hell, but I will die here unless something is done very soon. I lie on my back and hit the door with both legs. It doesn't give. I try again. Nothing.

I drink the last drops from my water bottle. This is the end of the line. I will never see Annie now. I will never see my family again.

The door opens. It's the manager. He helps me out. The comrades of my brigade stand shoulder to shoulder, smirking.

"Nothing's wrong with a bit of hazing," Petruha says. "You've been to the army, haven't you?"

"They kept me here until I passed out," Victor says.

"You've done a great job, Alex," the manager says. "The thermocouple works now like a champ."

I go to the bathroom and soak my head under the stream of cold water for a long while. When it's time for lunch, I find that my bologna sandwiches were stolen. I take a bus home. To hell with five kopecks. A man behind me sings an aria from *Aida*. He's either drunk or just got a new job someplace. I wish him nothing but luck. We, semi-Americans, are free and generous people. Even when we are hungry, which almost never happens.

Stazione del Grande

IT's 1980. I am thirty. I'm leaving the country of my birth. I'm a rootless cosmopolitan now. Stalin is probably just bones and scraps of rotten clothing, despite all the embalmment they pumped into him prior to his burial. The train that carries my family and a hundred other refugees comes to a stop at a tiny station outside Rome. The wind flip-flops the laundry on the balcony of an apartment house above us. Women's panties here are tinier and frillier than what they sell in Russia. Either the Italian women have smaller butts or they are not afraid to show them off.

"The problem is not that you're lucky," Volodya told me before I left him behind. "I could live with that. That even makes me happy. The problem is that I'm unlucky. They could've easily declared that my work wasn't classified as military research. They said that your work was civilian. It's totally random. Just like a lottery."

He's a *refusnik*. The pharaohs in charge won't let him and his wife Sylvia go no matter how hard he tries.

"It's dialectics," I said, averting my eyes, because I had nothing else to say. I've never won a lottery before and I probably never will again.

When we left our home city, on the border with Romania, we had to travel east first. We arrived to Moscow, changed trains and came back to Chop, a small village on the Soviet-Czechoslovakian border, about a hundred kilometers north from the starting point. At Chop railroad station, in the evening, they asked us to get off the train and wait for customs, which were in operation only in the mornings. We slept on the wooden benches, next to a large family of Gypsies. Mosquitoes buzzed, and bare light bulbs swayed above our heads.

In the morning, we stood in a grim line for customs. A boy of five was bicycling around the hall. I was surprised no one shot him. When our turn came, the customs officials weighed our belongings, and asked us to sacrifice either the cooking pots or our daughter's potty-chair. We chose the chair. At the door to the train, a soldier barred my daughter, and no one but her, with the barrel of his AK-47.

"*Documenti,*" he barked. I observed his zits, the whiskers he missed when shaving, the eyes mad with carefully induced hatred, mixed in equal proportion with zeal, and averted my eyes. I handed him my papers as he requested.

While he was examining them, I stared down at his well-polished jackboots, unable to face him anymore. He let us through. Outside, the train was surrounded with soldiers holding leashed German shepherds. They barked.

We boarded. An older woman fell under the weight of her suitcase. The soldiers laughed. I looked out of the window, and swore to never come back.

I begin to breathe again only when we crossed the Austrian border.

"The Italians are afraid for our safety," my wife says now. "They are good people. Always speak their mind."

I nod. The good people will put us on buses, as if international or domestic terrorists, who for some reason might be interested in us, couldn't blow up a bus as easy as they might a train. Actually, since most people here are Jews, the reason is easy to find. Then more good people will drive us into the city. They will let us stay there while the Americans review our applications for refugee status. The Americans will probably approve since they are also good people and since they hate bad people in the Soviet government. That's what we tell our daughter. She is two, but she understands everything. That's what she says.

Lorenzo, the Italian coordinator, comes into our car. "Hurry, hurry," he says in English. They assume that while the Russians can't speak Italian, they all speak English. I do.

"Sandro," Lorenzo tells me, though it's not my name. "You need to carry all your luggage to the door. *Pronto!* Translate it into your barbaric language." He giggles to indicate that this was a joke.

Lorenzo is a great guy, *un bravo ragazzo.* His head is shaven and square, and his chin is shaped like a brick. An inky mustache, the same color as his shirt, is attached under his Roman legionnaire nose. His grin is as wide as the rail tracks, and he wears dark glasses. When he took them off once, I saw his eyes, huge like the ripening olives. He stands with his hands on his hips, watching me carrying my own luggage and the stuff of the elderly couple who share our compartment.

He encourages me with his *prontos* and energetic finger clicking. He told me that he votes for the fascist party.

"*Communisto, no,*" he said. "Communism is bad. Mussolini was good for Italy. He fought the Mafia." He rolled his eyes to confirm that. He also told me he is Jewish but I don't believe him. Anyone can claim this.

Outside, the Italian sun is as round and warm as Lorenzo's smiling face. A large sign over the ticket counter says "Stazione del Grande." My daughter stares at a cop in a peaked cap, a pistol strapped to his white belt, and cries just in case. She is two. She can do what she wants. The cop yawns. His mouth is cavernous. He's doing his job, and we should be grateful to him for protecting us.

The buses are coming, each driven by a shaven-headed *un bravo ragazzo* with a brick-like chin, each dressed in a black shirt. We are lucky to have them on our side.

We arrive in Rome. Lorenzo helps us to find an apartment. The three bedrooms are shared by three families, two Russian and one Polish, in addition to an Italian landlady, Donna Lucia, who communicates with us by waving her hands and screaming. She was an opera singer in her youth. It's a communist-voting neighborhood. Outside our windows, kids are playing soccer and shouting. In the neighboring fascist district, they do the same.

We wait for our American visas. We need a sponsor who will support and cherish us while we are looking for a job.

Meanwhile, I work as a translator at the society that helps Russian immigrants. Lyuba is a homemaker. Every other day, we take a bus to the open market to buy groceries. We discover how to ride a bus without paying the fare. My wife learns the Italian words for meat and cheese. *Formaggio e carne.* Our daughter learns the word for ice cream. It's *gelato.* I learn the words for naked woman and making love: *donna nudo* and *faccia l'amore.*

One day in August, the American embassy requests the pleasure of our presence. The three of us take a bus, and we pay the fare this time. I put on a tie for the first time since leaving the Soviet Union. My wife and our daughter wear long dresses of identical style and fabric. We are a cute and respectable family that everyone wants to love.

The embassy building is heavily guarded. Everyone is afraid of *Brigate Rosse*, the Red Brigades. The woman in charge tells us that Rienville, New York, will take us. The job market is good there, and they look forward to a young, respectable family. Rienville is a very poetic name, with a hint of French. I check it on the map. It sits smack on the Pennsylvania border. Pennsylvania also sounds poetic, though I'm suspicious about borders. I wonder if I will be able to travel to Philadelphia to gaze at the Liberty Bell.

That evening we have a dinner of *formaggio e carne* and *gelato*. Donna Lucia appears, bangs her fist on the table, and yells, *"Soldi, soldi!"* I guess it's a gentle reminder that we need to pay the rent before we depart.

When our daughter falls asleep, I embrace the *donna nudo* and proceed with *faccia l'amore*. Behind the partition, the Polish couple abuse the springs of their mattress. They are going to Chicago. The future looks as bright as the silver dollar that the embassy woman gave to our daughter. Except that on the back of the coin there is a tiny scratch in the shape of the letter X. It means treasure is buried someplace.

The next day, Donna Lucia knocks at our door. *"Una telefonata per te,"* she says. She should have used the more polite form, *"una telefonata per lei,"* but I'm just a lowly tenant. And she did knock. She could have cut our throats while we slept or thrown acid in our faces.

I follow her to the master bedroom to pick up the phone. It's the only phone in the apartment. The door to the master bedroom is always locked, and she wears the key between her sagging breasts. I wouldn't get it out of there for all the antiques of Rome.

"Alex, we are already in Vienna." It's my mother.

Donna Lucia stands next to me, her arms folded on her chest. She is the guardian angel of her possessions. What is there to steal? An alabaster figurine of Eros with an erected penis? A wooden clock with one handle? A few faded photographs?

"Welcome to the free world," I say to my mother. "You'll like Vienna. And then you'll love Rome. And then we'll all love America. We are going to buy mansions next to each other and come to each other for breakfast. Three mansions. One for you. One for me. And one for Volodya."

"Talking about America," she says. "We have news for you, Alex. Your father and I decided to go to Israel instead."

I feel as if I'm choking on my own tongue and saliva. Is this a KGB plot of some kind?

"I know it may come as a surprise for you," my mother says, "but we think it's better this way."

A surprise? I want to say, you mean as a new toy car or a microscope on my birthday?

"You are not going to America?" I say.

"No. Sorry."

"Why Israel?" I say. "Speaking kitchen Yiddish doesn't make you Jewish. Neither does a 'Jew' word in your passport."

"What is he saying, Minnie?" I can hear my father in the background.

"We have to do it, Alex," she says. "We have no choice."

"Since when have you become Zionists? Or religious?" I ask.

"Tell him, Minnie," my father is saying in the background. "It's OK. Even if they overhear us."

"Who will overhear you?" I shout. "You are in Austria! A free country."

Donna Lucia purses her lips, but says nothing. I'm sure she doesn't understand a word of Russian. I already cursed her under my breath several times to test this theory.

"We think that Volodya will have a better chance to get out of the country if we are in Israel," my mother says. "We can start a campaign to save him. We will unite the whole country behind us."

"We can run the same campaign in America."

"Americans are not that interested. They have better things to do."

"Mom! This is so not true. Please, let me explain."

"Sorry, son. We know better."

"Good news and bad news," I'm telling Lyuba when I'm back to our room. She covers her mouth with her hands. Her eyes are so big that there is no room on her face for anything else. Seeing her, Mila begins to cry. Lyuba picks her up.

"They are going to Israel."

"Israel? Who is going to Israel?"

"My parents. So they could start a campaign to save Volodya. They will unite the whole country behind them. Because Americans don't care. Say good-bye to three mansions next to each other."

"I don't understand what you are talking about."

I wish I could help her. I wish someone could help me. I wish someone could pick me up before I start crying. But it's too late for that. It's so late that no amount of begging will change it.

Fire Drill

IT'S 1981, and I'm thirty-one.

It's ninety degrees outside, but I'm so cold that I would probably not register on infrared film, just like a polar bear. Though I'm dressed in my Saturday best, the thin layer of wool is not enough protection against the air conditioner set to resemble the Siberian winters of my childhood.

I sit in a windowless room across the steel desk from my interrogator. In the beginning, he introduced himself, but I didn't catch his name. Now, I've noticed the nametag I missed before. It says Fred Wilkinson. He wears a black polyester suit and tie, and a crisp white shirt. His graying hair is plastered on his egg-shaped head. I can't see his shoes under the table, but I suspect they are so polished that a man could use them as a shaving mirror, which, judging by his nicks and missed whiskers, he might have done.

Fred grills me for an hour. Then he hands me over to Archie Smith and leaves the room. Another hour passes. Next comes Bud Smolenski. Then Fred returns. This looks like a typical, time-proven, morale-breaking interrogation technique, but instead of getting a jail term, I might, just might, get a job.

"Where did you learn English so well?" they all ask. "It's fantastic."

Fantastic? You have no clue what the word means. It would really be fantastic if you hire me, I think.

"I studied it in school," I say. I didn't want to say that I self-studied English and still do. What if he prefers formal education and degrees? If you studied your English the way they taught us, I think, you'd be lucky to have a janitorial job. "I'm good with languages. Just a natural talent. I'm a fast learner and a team player."

Back home, I had no idea of the purchasing power of the American dollar. When I studied economics in the early seventies, rumor had it that a qualified autoworker in Detroit got $300 a month. That was the only cold fact I knew about the American income. A couple of years later, at my first engineering job, I was making 125 rubles a month. Lyuba, a physician, was making 100 rubles. Two hundred twenty-five rubles could carry a family from month to month, but barely.

After a few weeks in America, I begin to understand the reality of the local currency, but when Fred returns, makes me an offer and says, "$30,000 a year," my first thought is that the dollar is worth much less then I imagined. But I will take the offer, of course. Later, Fred tells me that it was the first time ever in his experience working for the HAL Corporation that they made someone an offer on the spot. I don't think I'm that good. I just lucked out. Or they were under the influence. After all, there are a lot of chemicals here, and engineers can always find a creative use for them.

My wife—who hasn't found a job yet—has the same reaction I did when I tell her the news.

"You're lying," she says. Our daughter Mila looks at us but says nothing. She's not even four, and she's entitled to keep her opinion to herself.

I wish I could show them tangible proof but the HAL people didn't give me an official letter.

"Dear Lyuba, my love," I say in the soothing voice she hates. "How can I prove it to you? Do you want parchment with wax seals? Or maybe a clay tablet?"

Truth be told, I'm not sure myself anymore. Maybe I dreamed it all up. I've done things like that before. I should have wired myself and recorded the whole thing.

"Not funny," my wife says. Mila shakes her head. She apparently doesn't think that I'm being funny either. What can I say? I've tried my best.

A month later, I stand in the underground lab at HAL, watching how the embedding machine is laying an insulated wire on the printed circuit board. It's a new type of machine, computer-controlled. I feed it eight-inch floppy disks with instructions. I have to evaluate its usefulness for the HAL Corporation. So far, it's not very useful. Too slow, though the wiring pattern is aesthetically pleasing. I won't mention the aesthetics in my report.

"A man with a real college degree," my colleague John, who stands next to me, says in a dramatic whisper to Fred Wilkinson. "A great addition to the company."

John's last name and his looks are real Italian but, unlike the Italian Italians, he speaks English with what sounds to me like a perfect American accent.

Fred, John's and my boss, nods. He looks pleased that John has confirmed his judgment of my degree and me. What am I to say? I can't express myself in English in front of management eloquently anyway, even if I know what to say. And what is the point of a speech if it's not eloquent?

Fred is pushing sixty. He is bold and mustachioed but not yet that wrinkled. John tells me that Fred is from the old school of management with only a high school diploma. They used to seep into management by osmosis. Twenty years in the ranks, and then—a promotion. Fred pats me on the back and leaves me in John's capable hands.

John has a bachelor's. He's my age and not married. He has a steady girlfriend.

We all wear white shirts and ties. John told me that a few years ago every engineer at HAL wore a jacket at all times. And before that, they wore hats and sang the company's anthem every morning before work.

> *Always forward, always forward,*
> *always forward H-A-L!*

I wish they still did that. I love to sing along, though, as the Russian saying goes, a bear stepped on my ear.

John is a rebel. His shirt is short-sleeved. I tell him about my three-month stay in Italy. His parents came from Naples, but he has never been outside the Northeastern United States.

I say, "They claim that there is much terrorism in Italy. I saw no terrorism."

He nods, looking sidewise as if I am transparent. Maybe I am.

"No terrorism at all?" he finally asks.

"No terrorism," I confirm. I expect him to shower me with questions about Russia and Italy. Instead he says, "No terrorism, huh?" He tells me he doesn't read books. Only the newspaper and trade magazines. His dream is to buy a cottage on a lake. He likes water, and the land prices are always going up. He's been to New York City, a three-hour drive away, once, as a child, when his parents took him to a ball game. The game and the hot dogs were good, but he hated the traffic, the noise, the pollution and the congestion.

"Back in Russia," I say, "they think that America is dangerous. They think people get robbed on the streets. I do not see that. Americans are very generous. And they are rich. Rich people do not rob other rich people."

John feeds the machine another floppy disk. He's a busy man who doesn't have time for idle talk. But who will I talk to besides him? He is the only one I see all day, and when I come home there's only my wife and daughter.

"Italian ice cream is the best in the world," I say. "Have you ever tried it? We used to buy one cone for the three of us because we couldn't afford more. Once, I saw a whole container in the store. For five hundred liras. It's like fifty cents. Cheap. I wanted to buy it, but they said it was five hundred liras off. The sale price. Funny, huh?"

"We have great ice cream here, too," he says without turning. "Pat Mitchell's Homemade Ice Cream."

"How about coffee?" I say. "I will buy you coffee."

He always finds time for coffee when I buy it for him. It's a quarter a cup. I hate to throw the empty cups out but everyone does it.

"Sure," he says.

We walk down the aisle. Tom, the technician who takes care of the embedding machine by lubricating, aligning and sacrificing babies to it, joins us. He wears a blue lab coat over his jeans and a checkered shirt. Technicians are free men; they need no ties or white shirts. Of course, they are paid less than the engineers. Tom's head is always lowered as if he were playing a serious game where someone might get bloody, and his eyes shine with unquenchable fire from their deep sockets. John told me once that a man banged Tom's new car, and that Tom broke his jaw. I knew that Americans like their cars, but I didn't realize they like them that much.

My feet move cautiously on the worn linoleum over the concrete. Naked pipes, some the size of my fist, some the size of my head, run alongside the walls. They don't remind me of snakes because they are clearly not alive and never have been alive. The fluorescent lights flicker overhead. John looks like a Zombie, and probably so do I. Mary Chizevsky and Fred stand by the machine. They also look like Zombies. Mary is the only female engineer in the project.

She's a gorgeous femme to die for if you are into dying. Short spiky hair, padded shoulders, pleated skirt, high heels with a slightly pointy toe, bloody nails, rimmed eyes and smeared lipstick. She's thin and flat as an ironing board that has been compressed by a steamroller. Very fatale. She joined us last week and she does chores. Drives to pick up parts, sorts purchased components, draws organizational charts and files the documentation. She doesn't brew coffee, though, because she's a human being and not a machine. That's what she purportedly said.

We, the five Zombies in the industrial setting, chat, exchanging how-are-yous and what's-ups.

"You know Mary, right?" Fred asks me.

"I met her in your cabinet," I say.

They laugh. They don't know that "cabinet" means "office" in Russian, and I am too embarrassed to explain. My English skills are not up to snuff yet.

Mary doesn't laugh. She lowers her eyes. Her cheeks turn red. A curious reaction for a Zombie.

"I'll buy drinks for everyone," I suggest, saying it loudly so that everyone will understand and won't mistake my words for something else. Loudness is the key to clarity when you speak with an accent.

"Drinks?" Fred laughs again. "Too early for that."

"I mean coffee."

"Atta boy," Fred says, pocketing the change he was holding in his hand. Most people here are so happy when they save a quarter or two. By now, I know that a quarter is not too much so it's got to be something else. They probably are happy to allow you to perform an act of selfless charity.

John told me that Fred is filthy rich. John told me that Fred's father bought HAL shares for sixty cents a piece early in the century. They kept splitting, and he never sold them. He just kept pocketing the dividends. Now, Fred inherited it all. He's a millionaire and could live on the dividends alone, but he continues working because he's having fun. You can't tell by observing his face, which looks like it is constantly chewing on a rotten lemon. But people have different ideas of what fun and the pursuit of happiness is. This is America.

I drop my coins in the machine, let everyone pick their cups, and then sip the scalding, overly sweet liquid. I hate coffee, but I'd sacrifice anything for friendship. Everybody turns non-verbal for a while, pursuing the machine-produced happiness.

We hear the piercing voice of an alarm and I almost drop my cup.

"It's a drill," Fred says. "But we gotta go outside. I hope it doesn't rain."

"They never do drills on rainy days," John says.

I sniff the air for any traces of bitter almonds. They use a lot of chemicals here, after all. I smell nothing except bitter coffee. We go outside. It rains. The sidewalk is full of people with HAL badges. I've just learned that they call them zipper-heads. It means that the bosses can open their heads at any point, and insert or remove information. Two fire trucks are flashing their lights next to the exit. Black smoke comes out from one of the windows. It smells acrid and sharp. It looks like a very realistic drill. Someone has spent a lot of time to prepare it. I half-expect to hear Mr. Orlov from my Russian past bark commands.

We walk to the parking lot, our evacuation point. Rain drenches my white shirt and collects in my cup. Mary's eyeliner is floating down her cheeks.

I hear a muffled explosion. Someone hits me in the back and I go down. I see my cup flying in front of me. I fall on something softer than asphalt. It's Fred. I've never been on top of a millionaire before and I don't like it a bit. He's bony. He also wiggles. In addition, I scraped my hands on the asphalt because that was where they landed.

I rise and help him get up. His eyes are glossy and a thin stream of blood flows down from a cut in his forehead. His white shirt is stained from hitting the pavement. We are surrounded by dazed zipper-heads. Some of them are bloody, but not overly so. Mary has no blood on her, but she screams. No one seems to be poisoned. Nothing like back home, at the Sunshine Chemical plant. This is America, after all. Nothing drastic can happen at an American industrial company. This is the land of safety regulations and managerial benevolence. Big brother, lawyers and trade unions always insert a soft cushion under your tush when you fall. They are watchful and swift.

"Some drill, huh?" I say to Fred, wiping blood and grime from my face. The rain helps.

"It's not a drill," John shouts. "It's for real."

Fred mouths something. He probably didn't understand what I said. As I mentioned before, my English skills are not up to snuff yet and if you are a millionaire, you don't need to be that attentive. So I repeat myself, only louder this time. I practically shout it, though my throat and chest hurt. As I said, when you speak a foreign language, loudness is always helpful. Besides, you can only be loud when you're alive.

Writer

It's 1985. I am thirty-five. If you like literature, and you have failed as a politician and movie actor, where would you look for your next pursuit? While the answer may lie on the surface in its leisurely splendor, what do you do about the obvious complication: the language barrier? I've always been jumpy, but this leap looks too difficult considering that I only began learning English in earnest five years ago, at the age of thirty, and am running out of stride space. And what kind of writer can you be without command of the language? A shitty one, usually. Except if this writer is me.

I write:

"The police officer, a captain, John Smith, kissed the pretty woman Antoinette Van Der Hoot (with flying red hair on the top of her head) on her big mouth, and she returned his kiss with abandon suitable for a nineteenth-century Hawaiian maiden. They both jumped into the bed and got separated from their underwear in the practiced motions of accomplished undressers who get paid not by the hour, but by the amount of work done."

Writing in a second language is supposed to be a torture. But I enjoy it. Maybe I'm a masochist. Maybe I need to see a shrink. It could be fun. She would put me on a couch and ask if my mother liked to communicate with me in writing.

Even though I enjoy writing in general, I struggle with the grammar. The Russian language has no articles. It's a matter of philosophy. There is no "a door" or "the door" in Russian. Just "door." Who cares if that door has been already mentioned? If it's really important, we say "that very door" or something like that.

I put the story in an envelope, include a self-addressed stamped envelope and send it to *The New Yorker*. They say no.

After I'm done pulling out my hair, I buy a book on the writing craft. I read Margaret Atwood and T. C. Boyle. I listen to how my neighbors, coworkers and people in the grocery line talk.

I see an ad for a writer's group meeting at the local bookstore. Should I go? I'm ashamed of my accent. I mean, it's OK for an engineer to speak with an accent. It's sometimes even to his advantage—it could mean he's smart. But would they laugh at the guy who can't even speak the language and yet wants to compete against the finest writers in the nation?

In the end, shame is not a strong enough force to stop me. I go. At the entrance to the store, I pass by the table with the new fiction. I have to stop. One day, I say to myself, my book will be here. A woman who browses a paperback with a sultry lady on the cover, looks at me as if she can read my mind, and not only is sure that I'm crazy, but that no physician could ever help me.

Five writers sit around a table with a pile of books on it: four women in their fifties and sixties and a man of about my age. I sit next to him so that the women won't think I am hitting on them. I wish.

"My name is Alex, and I'm a writer," I say. I've rehearsed this ice-breaking opening in the mirror until finally I'm happy with it.

But the ice stays solid. They don't laugh. As a matter of fact, only one of them even looks at me. The rest stare into notebooks that probably contain the next best-selling American novel. Four must-read novels. I will be busy soon.

"I just said the same thing," the man says. "They didn't laugh either."

"Your name is Alex, too?"

"I'm Albert," he says.

We shake hands. The women ignore us. One of them reads from her notebook:

The curvaceous blonde embraces Robert's wide, muscular shoulders as if she were a housewife on a budget who just won $56.77 at a slot machine in Vegas and he were a token-selling boy.

"Oh, Robert, my eternal love," she exclaims forlornly, her full breasts jumping up and down like two maidens ready for a ball, but whose mother is too strict to let them out. Her crimson dress with a low bodice clings to her shapely legs, firm thighs and seductive spine like the skin of a snake that just molted. "How heartbreaking it is to myself to let you go!"

"But I am obliged to take my leave, Cassandra," the handsome gentleman vociferates desperately. "My duty to my country! My love to yourself! They tear my body and my soul into two equally anxious but lovingly hopeful parts."

The other women clap and vociferate: "Lovely, lovely, Nadine!"

I look at Albert. Albert looks at me. We get up and leave. Nadine glares at us, but her colleagues hardly notice.

"There is a pizzeria next door," Albert says. "Brother Giuseppe. My treat."

The dark cloud showers us as if we were mortal readers instead of divine writers. When we've killed a pizza and a two-liter bottle of Coke, Albert reads his poem.

The Land Is Silent

Perhaps she forgot
the wet eyes of the rich
she could often disregard
and the loud Yes
of the Paltry's Captain
while she seeped from his mouth,
and solemn knives dragging
across her clothing,
and clean grass bringing back to life
her animals, her blood,
invigorating her mind.
She forgot the easygoing new villages
and rubber motor planes,
flown by lively minds
and Russian train cars with birthing beds,
solidly built,
with paper bills, crystals and noise,
that open under her feet.
Forgetting it all,
she laughs like a whore, shamefully.

I'm devastated. I'll never be able to write like that. What can I say in the presence of a master? He's a mighty river, and I'm a parched desert. He's a tall tree, and I'm a stunted bush. He's a roaring lion, and I'm a cowering kitten. I should sell my word processor and bury my quill.

"This is good," I say. "Very good."

I'm waiting for him to ask me to read, but he doesn't. I tell him the story of my coming to America instead. Though he doesn't interrupt, I try to run through it as fast as I can, so not to usurp his time.

"It surely beats my poem," he says when I'm done.

Not only does he listen, but he appreciates. I'm so delighted that I'm ready to embrace him.

"We should meet again," I say.

"Sure thing," he says. "Good writers should stick together."

I know we will. Like two Velcro strips.

The following day, I write:

"'Your life flashes before your eyes when you die, right?' Cody said, rocking in the chair, a Kmart special that his wife Amber had given him for his sixtieth a year before. 'It's flashed three times already on account of breakfast. And five times the day before. Maybe I'm gonna die soon. You reckon?'

'Hell if I know,' Chip said. 'You're th' smart one.'

Cody had taken out a kitchen chair for him, and Chip kept trying to rock on it without much success.

A crow cawed in the poplar above them and sunshine edged toward Cody's bare feet, which were the color of sour milk. Veins popped up here and there, roots of a strange tree."

I put the story in an envelope, include a self-addressed stamped envelope and send it to *Really Unknown Writer*. The editor writes, "Cool shit." I guess this means he likes it. He sends me a copy of the magazine. My story is embellished with a picture of a man in overalls carrying a shotgun in one hand and a heavy book in the other.

I tell my wife. She's heavily pregnant. She's happy for me. I tell my eight-year-old Mila. She thinks it's cool. I call my brother back home. The pharaohs are still refusing his exit visa.

"You wrote a story in English, huh?" he says. He tells me about Gorbachev who just came to power. He says that people put a lot of hope in him. But my brother considers going to Israel. If they let him.

"You're no Zionist," I say. "What are you going to do in Israel? You don't speak Hebrew. You're not even circumcised."

"I want to join our parents. They fought for me over all these years. And you don't speak English well either."

"Not true."

"It's true."

What kind of writer am I if I can't convince him?

The following day, while driving to work on the bridge over the Susquehanna River and listening to NPR, I make the most important discovery of my writing career: Don't use two words if you can get away with one. I don't know what inspires me. Is it the poem they recite on the radio, or a young woman flicking a cigarette out of the window of a passing car, or perhaps a dry leaf blowing across my windshield? Whatever it is, I'm grateful.

Of course, since the editors pay per word, a minimalist isn't paid as much as a writer who uses a great abundance of stunningly beautiful words, but this is not a concern for me now.

I write a story about a man who made it in a foreign country. A man like the Biblical Lot who made it in Sodom. I call him Ariel. I write about Ariel buying a mansion in the suburb of a large city. Ariel gets married and has two daughters. He is prosperous. He buys cars and fire insurance. His daughters are engaged. One day, two strangers come to his house and ask him to wash their feet. He calls the cops. The cops handcuff the strangers and throw them into a car headfirst. The next day, Ariel buys insurance against brimstones. His neighbors like him. The only cloud on his horizon is that his wife puts too much salt in his food. He's one happy immigrant.

I don't send this story out because I'm afraid. Fearful reflections, that's what we writers do well. Good writers, bad writers. Even the ones who fail at the language barrier because they run out of stride space.

The following week, my brother calls me.

"Sylvia and I decided to go to America after all," he says. "When the pharaohs let us."

"Mazeltov, Volodya," I say. I'm happy. We, writers, have more acute emotions than the general population. When we are happy, we write. So I write this haiku:

> *Pharaoh let us go*
> *because he had no choice.*
> *Why aren't we happy?*

Really, why? I should ask Albert when I see him next.

The Voting Machine

It's 1986. I am thirty-six. Today I have a choice: an ass or an elephant. I prefer cats to the rest of the animal kingdom, but the cat is not on the ballot, and I'm not sure that I can write her in. They say that all candidates are fat cats, but I don't believe in this subversive lie. This is my first election since coming to America, and I take it as seriously as I can.

I walk into the fire station, my designated voting place. I'm ready to yell "Where is the fire?" but I'm afraid they will get confused by my accent and misunderstand my good-natured folksy cheering. Four white-haired ladies are manning the tables. It appears that in voting, just like in the cleaning business, only ladies are running the show. I guess the lords are bowling or watching TV at home.

I announce my name, holding out my eagle-adorned, freshly minted, blue-and-gold passport, but they don't ask me for identity proof. They let me vote for the county clerk, the town mayor, and the family judge without making sure that I am who I claim to be. I'm pissed. What if an imposter wants to take over my hard-earned voting right? But I don't want to make an ass of myself. I'm voting Republican.

First of all, the Republicans are against the Communism. Second, they are for law and order. Third, they will lower my taxes. They are as important to me, the student of democracy, as the pupil of my eye. I know what to do. I'm a mean voting machine, and I will make sure my candidates get my aye. As they say, an aye for an eye.

I enter the booth, pull the lever, and close the curtain. I feel like I stand in a temple of Democracy. I'm full of awe, as if Lady Liberty herself is breathing in my ear (her breath is mint-flavored) and makes the back of my head smolder with her torch.

I pull down the pointers next to my candidates' names, exposing red letter Xs. It's symbolic. X marks the spot of the Democrats' defeat. Let the best elephant win. I pull the lever to register my votes and to open the curtain, but the lever is stuck. I can't move it.

What do I do? I know for sure that head scratching and cursing help very little. I turn to Lady Liberty for advice, but she's mum. She just shrugs, as if shrugging has ever helped anyone. Is she a closet Democrat? I pull again, with both hands. My muscles strain against the load of democracy, free choice and citizen's obligation, but it doesn't budge. Foul play at play.

I should ask for help in a more assertive way. Or be more eloquent. Or appeal to her sense of duty. But how can you be any of the above with someone who is made of copper?

I don't have much experience with flesh-and-blood American women. At work, I'm surrounded by males. Mary Chizevsky, the only woman-engineer we had, has long gone for pastures friendlier to females. We have a few American house friends, but the women in the couples are just like Russians to me. Some of them even took Russian in college. So real American women are a mystery. I even crafted a poem about them:

> American woman,
> You are a face in the fog
> That stares at me from the sidewalk
> When I walk at night
> Only your eyes are bright,
> American woman.

Now, I'm about to get down on my knees and crawl out, but the presence of Lady Liberty, a woman (albeit a green one), deters me. The draperies are, symbolically, her gown. What would the white-haired ladies think when they see a family man crawling under a woman's dress, even in the metaphysical sense? No one talked about this situation in citizenship class, though they covered so many esoteric topics that a lady from Guatemala and a lord from Egypt fell asleep and snored delicately on more than a single occasion. Though I always sat in the first row, I never missed anything behind me either. I guess that was one of the reasons why they chose me to deliver the acceptance speech when they granted us citizenship. I made a great speech. Everyone was moved.

I'm not a damned Communist or any other type of pervert. I'm a law-abiding citizen, and I pay my taxes, though they collect too much for the benefit of the work-refusniks.

I should use my newly acquired American ingenuity. I will yell for help and the cavalry will come to the rescue. I breathe in a lungful of free American air. I open my capitalist mouth. Both Lady Liberty and I will be safe without getting embarrassed. And then we might even sue the board of elections. This is the American way. Whoever doesn't like it, can go back to the old country and complain to the United Nations, that global nest of pinko sympathizers. And then they would wait the rest of their natural lives for the exit visa to leave the country, just like I did. And if they were as lucky as my brother, they would wait forever. And nothing is longer than forever.

Fishing for Men

IT's 1987. I am thirty-seven. Boris is a man formerly from Odessa, now from Cleveland. He looks large even inside this cavernous terminal. He just introduced himself and shook my hand with the force of a gale wind mixed with heavy rain. We sit next to each other on the world's most uncomfortable bench. My flight is delayed, and so is his. Every flight is delayed or canceled. Human misery hangs low like a thundercloud, and peoples' outbursts punctuate it like thunderclaps.

Ten minutes ago, I was cursing fate for getting stuck here. Now, not only am I stuck, but I'm next to Boris. My wife says life comes in light and dark patches. I didn't know I was in a light patch ten minutes before. Why did he fish me out from the crowd?

Boris takes a pen out of the pocket of his double-breasted suit, and draws crude figures on a sheet of paper: three men, one on top of the other, each progressively smaller than the one before. All three have hatchet noses and big ears. They could be brothers. The three stooges. Or they could have come from a Julius Streicher newspaper cartoon, circa nineteen-thirties. *"Der Stürmer: "Die Juden sind unser Unglück!"* The Jews are our misfortune.

"American Jews on the bottom," Boris explains in heavily accented English, "then Russian Jews, and then Jews from Odessa. That's the levels of smartness. Learn and be thankful. Got it?"

"Sounds like a pyramid scheme," I say in Russian.

"Scheme, shmim. You know I'm right," he continues in English. Some people want to impress everyone, even perfect strangers.

"Did you take drawing lessons in college?" I ask. "My dream was to draw a naked girl."

"See, you already proved my theory. The man in the middle. Not very smart."

"The Jewish religion is funny," he continues. "The Jews left Egypt because they didn't want to be slaves. Now, they are slaves to traditions and rituals no one fully understands."

I don't know why he thinks I'm religious. We haven't touched on this subject. How can you tell a person is religious unless you talk to him anyway? You can tell an observant person by his clothes or mannerism or whatnot. For example, observant Jews wear skullcaps and beards. Or observant Muslims wear beards and skullcaps. But you can't tell a religious person by looks alone. Religion is within, like the heart or liver. You spill your guts only when you talk.

"It's your religion, too," I say. "You're Jewish."

"I'm a militant atheist."

"What's the difference between a militant and a scientific atheist?"

A thunderclap drowns my words. Boris flinches. I suppress a smile.

Back in Russia, we all knew that religion was, as Marx said, the opium of the masses. That postulate presented problems to me. I didn't know anyone who smoked or otherwise ingested opium. I suspected that opium made someone either happy or relaxed. So, what was religion supposed to do to you, make you enjoy life or make you sleepy?

When I asked this question of my Scientific Atheism teacher in high school, he said that the textbook didn't discuss this. Judging by the speed of his answer, I surmised that he was taught in college that if a young boy of a Jewish background asks you something inappropriate, you should give him a sophisticated reply that would silence his curiosity rather than punching him in the nose.

"You said?" Boris asks now.

"Nothing." I pull a newspaper out of my briefcase, but the small time diversion doesn't deter him.

"A French philosopher said that Jewish religion is intolerable," Boris says.

"Voltaire. He said that Judaism is 'intrinsically inimical to personal conscience.' He also said that 'Christianity is the most ridiculous, the most absurd, and bloody religion that has ever infected the world.' He was a talkative guy. Just like you."

In my department, there are three born-again Christians. They'd love to convert me. That would be a heavenly gift from Jesus. They practically salivate when they see me. It's a hundred times better then saving a dolphin. When we go to the company's cafeteria together, they sit around the table with their eyes closed, bowing their heads and praying silently before touching the food. If I were more observant, I wouldn't even come to the cafeteria, though I select only Biblically permissible food. I also should say a benediction, *brachot*, but I don't feel comfortable doing it.

I ask why they don't eat Biblically proscribed food. Tom, the leader, explains that Jesus came to an apostle in a dream and allowed everyone to eat non-Kosher. I ask if the apostle had too much gefilte fish and Manischewitz the night before.

The trio doesn't laugh. They just stare at each other as if someone has just farted at the table. A few minutes later, Tom asks if I can eat spinach that touched celery. Now, the trio laughs. So do I. I love spinach.

Kosher food is a touchy subject. At the synagogue, a man named Abraham, a born-again Jew, tells a joke about an observant Jewish man who died and went to Heaven. He was offered all kinds of food, but asked, "Who is responsible for the kosher supervision here?" "God," was the answer. "Give me some salad," the man said. The joke is supposed to be funny because salad is kosher by definition.

Abraham is an expert on kosher food. As they say in Russia, he ate a dog on this subject. Before he became Abraham, his name was Robert, and he used to be a hippy. He still wears his hair long and just recently removed an earring. By the way, Abraham says that I am a heretic because I question everything. I say that Benedict Spinoza was a heretic as well. I wonder if he said *brachot* on food back in seventeenth-century Amsterdam.

"Voltaire was a talkative guy like me?" Boris says now. "You're funny. I like you."

I'm afraid he is going to say that he'd love to convert me to atheism. I pick up my briefcase, get up and go to the window. The rain is over. The sun is peeking out from the clouds. Way above, higher than any airplane route, higher than even the space ships, the observant Jewish man is having his kosher salad. Maybe he is even having a fish with scales and fins.

I wish I could talk to him now. I bet he has a lot to share. I would ask him if they have different sections for different religions in paradise, the way they divide some cemeteries. Do they have a section for people who have never made up their minds, or are they forced to sit on the fence?

How about people like Boris? I don't believe in hell because the eternity of torture is too cruel for my God, but they must have a separate section for Boris' ilk. Something similar to sitting in the back seat of a theater, behind a really tall man who smells of cigarettes and talks on his cell phone. I've seen spiders fighting each other in a glass jar once.

"Your eyes are glazed over, pal," Boris says. "Are you high or something?"

I didn't even notice that he stands next to me.

My daughter Mila started talking before she turned one, and memorized poetry before she was two. But when she went to a Jewish-community-based nursery school back in 1981, the kids called her yo-yo because she knew no English. She was four.

At home, she cried and my wife cried next to her. What does a man do when the two people closest to him suffer? I thought about the advice I could give, but I hated every one of them.

Once I said to Mila that a yo-yo is just a game. Would you cry if someone calls you soccer? Or chess? Or maybe Scrabble? You wouldn't do that, would you? Why is yo-yo any different? My wife said that it was a stupid remark, so they kept huddling together and crying. And I kept trying to invent a better remark, but failed. I really hated myself when I failed, so back then I hated myself every day.

One snowy winter afternoon, the father of one of my daughter's classmates stopped his car when I stood at the bus stop, lowered his window and offered to teach me Biblical Hebrew.

"How about some English instead?" I asked. I felt as if icicles were floating in the veins of my hands and feet. I held Mila in my hands because she was cold.

"You could learn English anywhere," he said. His son stuck out his tongue at us, and muttered, "yo-yos."

"I like Biblical Hebrew," I said. "I know what the Hebrew word for fish is, for example. *Dag*. But English is more useful now. It would help me find a job. Wouldn't you agree, sir?"

The father shrugged and drove away. His son kept making faces in the back window until the car disappeared behind a curtain of snow.

Hebrew is a serious language. A being's name in Hebrew is its essence. That's why Adam had to name every creature in the Bible. I'm sure the man and his son meant well. I should call them Oil and Vinegar. Or Yin and Yang. Or Big Dipper and Little Dipper.

"Why didn't he give us a ride?" Mila asked.

"He's a busy American."

I could get a ride anywhere, I added under my breath. I don't need Oil for that.

"I wouldn't go with them," Mila says. "Brian is a meanie."

The bus comes and swallows us into its warm belly. The only other passenger, a bundled up older woman, eyes us suspiciously. Does she think we're going to bite her, or what?

"A nice lady gave mommy and me a ride once," Mila says. "She told us 'Only scum ride the bus.' What is scum, Daddy?"

"Scum is a foul layer that forms on the surface of a liquid."

"Phew. Does it stink?"

"Only if you corner it."

Now, at the airport, I turn to Boris, my former compatriot, my current fellow American, someone I might get buried next to if I'm very unlucky.

I'm ready to say that maybe an eternity of torture, or at least a few hundred years of it, is not such a bad idea, but the announcement over the intercom interrupts me.

"Flight 845 to Cleveland is now boarding."

"Here is my card," Boris says. "If you need a car, call me. Call me anyway. We'll chat. I still can make a man out of you."

I take the card. It's one of those you can print on your inkjet. It says, in English, "Boris Belinsky, Pre-Owned Car Salesman!!"

"What happened to your third exclamation point?" I want to ask, but I grin, business-like, instead.

"A man," I say, "is the product of the environment and genetics."

Maybe I will drive the next time instead of flying. When you fly, you are closer to heavens. But when you drive, you are all alone, except for God. He will never try to convert you. He is above fishing for men.

Annie!

It's 1988. I am thirty-eight. We are Americans now, transported by the magic of détente to the other side of the moon. Isn't that what I have always wanted? We drive from Rienville, New York, to Orlando. One thousand, one hundred and fifty miles inside a Volvo station wagon to meet Uncle Michael and his kids. They live in walking distance from each other, a rarity for Americans. Russian blood for sure. When I called before departing, I spelled Pittsburgh for him, but didn't ask if Annie is married. She's thirty now, so she probably is. Did the years wipe out her smile? They didn't wipe out my wife's.

Too bad my brother and my parents can't come. They are not Americans, and the trip here is too difficult.

We stay overnight at a small inn in South Carolina. I toss on a narrow, lumpy mattress. My wife shares the other bed with our daughters. The three of them combined weigh less than I do alone, so it's OK. I'm thinking nonsense. If the human body is a symbiosis of cells, as I read in a science journal recently, what happens if they recognize this one day and leave? All of humanity will become empty suits, dresses and uniforms.

The next day, we drive again. As usual, I listen to the girls yelling in the back seat: "She's poking me in the eye! In the eye." I raise the volume on the radio.

"At least we have daughters to yell," my wife comments. "There are people who would kill for a healthy child. And we have two."

She's right, of course. I wish I were so logical. Or so saintly.

In the afternoon, we reach Orlando. The kids want to go to Disney *now.*

Uncle Michael sits in the shade, on a bench outside of his apartment building. He had a stroke recently, so when he gets up, he leans on a cane with a lion's head. He grins. We embrace. He doesn't smell of an old man, and I grin just like he does, inch for inch.

"Come inside," he says. "You must be hungry. I'll introduce you to Baby. Annie's here, too. With her brood. Lennie couldn't make it. He's playing golf."

Brood, huh? Well, what did I expect? A Vestal Virgin? I've never exchanged a single word with her, except in my wet dreams. It's all my fault. But who is Baby? Lennie's wife?

We follow Uncle inside. His wife stands right next to the door, as if she has planned an ambush. Her ash-blonde hair clashes with her face, wrinkled by the Southern sun. She embraces us, too.

"That's Baby," Uncle says. "My Baby has diamonds in her eyes."

Right. On her neck, too.

Annie—it's got to be her—sits next to a fast-balding man about my age and a boy about ten. She gets up. Talk about diamonds—that's what she is, up to and including the Mona Lisa smile.

She embraces me, and I hold her a heartbeat longer than the situation calls for. I haven't embraced another woman for over ten years. My wife smells very peaceful, like home. Annie smells of an exotic flower, of a candlestick romance, of a moonless night. My wife and Annie Mona Lisa each other. The walls of the family room are framed with mirrors; they multiply our extended family over and over again. So many gems that a simple man like me can lose his eyesight.

Uncle seats me at the best place in the house—between him and Annie. She wears shorts, and so do I. When our knees meet momentarily, my cheeks turn red. I know that my wife sees it, but so far she is silent.

"How have you been, cousin?" Annie asks.

I want to tell her that I've been in love with her for the last twenty years. No, my entire life.

"I'm fine," I say. "How have you been?"

I hope she will say that though she has never seen me, she's been waiting for me at least for the last twenty years. That this balding man—I learned that his name is either Bernie or Barry—was a mistake or a substitute, like margarine for butter. But she informs me that she is fine as well.

Fine! I begin to hate this word. It sounds like a penalty.

We eat. Normally, I would be able to describe every dish we ate a week later, but now I'm hardly paying attention to what I put in my mouth. Baby does most of the talking. Unlike Mickey (that's Uncle, I guess), she is still working, in real estate.

"What do you do?" Annie asks me.

"I'm an engineer."

"Ah, a kindred spirit. I'm a math teacher."

But what if my interest lies beyond the spiritual? I glance at my wife, but she's talking to Barry or Bernie. Strangely, I'm not jealous as I always am when she talks with another man. The kids elbow each other silently.

After dinner, we move to the family room. Baby complains about the high cost of maintaining the apartment. Uncle asks about my father. I show him a few pictures I brought for this occasion.

When we part, I hold Annie's hand longer than is proper. I know that I will never see her again, because my wife said the car trip to Florida takes too long, and I won't be able to justify driving here alone.

But I forgot about that modern invention—airplanes. Three months later, my company sends me to Orlando for a business trip.

Packing my suitcase, I feel Lyuba's eyes on me.

"Don't spend too much time in the sun," she says. I promise I won't.

When I arrive, I call Annie. What will I say if her husband or son picks up the phone? But it's her.

"Alex!" She sounds happy to hear me, and my heart skips. Two hours later, I sit at a table in the restaurant across the street from my hotel, waiting for her. It's early evening, ninety-five degrees outside. The windows sweat, but I'm cold. I follow the slow movement of the second hand of my watch. I go through the same transformations a genie in a bottle does, but at an accelerated pace: at first, I'm ready to give Annie the moon and the stars. Half an hour later, I'm ready to kill her.

I get up when she finally arrives. My hands shake. My genie thoughts disappear like small chunks of ice on a hot stove. We embrace, but she pulls away too fast for me to savor it. We sit down.

"How are your wife and kids?" she asks. "Your parents? And your brother? You have a brother, right?"

"They are fine. How is Bernie?"

"Barry is great. Are you hungry?" she asks.

I want to say that I'm hungry for her, but I just shake my head. It seems like I've lost the gift of speech I thought I was so generously endowed with. The waitress approaches, and I'm about to shoo her away. Annie stops her and orders. I'm telling myself that I shouldn't be surprised. After all, people come to a restaurant to eat. I order the first thing my eyes focus on when I manage to look away from Annie's face.

"My father showed me your photograph when I was eleven," Annie says, after she takes a few sips from her ice water glass. I've never seen anyone drink so gracefully. That arc of the wrist, those neat and nimble fingers.

"It felt funny to have a cousin in Russia. Just like having a relative on the island of Madagascar. I almost had a crush on you. Isn't it silly?"

Father! He sent mail to the imperialists after all, risking everything. My silent hero.

I watch her eat. I have something in my mouth as well, but I don't know what it is and whether or not I chew it or swallow it whole.

"Why is it silly?" I finally ask.

"What? Oh, that childhood crush? I had crushes on many people then. Hormones, you know."

"I want to tell you so much," I say. "I dreamt about this conversation."

She pushes her empty plate away. "The steak was good. How was your chopped liver?"

The waitress re-appears. "Separate checks?" she asks. Is she dumb? Doesn't she know that Annie and I belong to each other?

"Yes, separate checks, please," Annie says.

I can't pull out my wallet because my hands shake.

"Call me when you're in Florida again," Annie says.

"May I call you before that?"

"Why?"

Why? That's a just question, milady. Because I need you, my love, I think. Because if we can't be together, at least I want to hear the sound of your voice. Because I've longed for you all my life.

"We are cousins, aren't we?" I say instead.

"Sure," she says. "Call me, cousin. Any time. I look forward to it."

I'm sure she means it. Otherwise, my world would collapse.

Back home, my wife asks how my trip was. I tell her it was fine and that I stayed out of the sun. She hugs me, but instead of enjoying her warmth, all I can do is wonder if she can smell Annie's perfume. No, that's silly. We embraced only for a second. If she does, she says nothing.

The next day, I call Annie.

"Ah, Alex," she says. "It's good to hear from you. How was your flight?"

I tell her all the details. How I was delayed for two hours, and that when we finally boarded I sat next to the Rienville chief of police. I share the chief's joke, trying to imitate his gruff voice. Annie laughs.

"Gee officer, that's terrific. The last officer only gave me a warning," she repeats. "It's so funny to imagine a police chief speaking with an accent."

The next week, I call her and tell her a Russian joke, "Q: What is a one word joke? A: "Communism."

She laughs again. "You're so funny, Cuz."

The following week I tell her that I keep dreaming about her. She pauses. "Where is the punch line?" she finally asks.

I'd better stick to jokes for now. When I'm done telling them, she tells me about books she's read, mostly romances. Sometimes she complains about her neighbors or work colleagues or her students. It doesn't matter. I relish the sound of her voice. Every call is the high point of my week, a peak. Every other day is just a valley.

I call my father to tell him about Uncle Michael and Annie.

"You should call him, Daddy," I say.

"I'm afraid we would have nothing to say to each other. We are totally different, he and I."

"You won't know unless you try."

"True."

As far as I know, he never calls.

Two and One Nights

IT'S STILL 1988. I am still thirty-eight. The drapes are drawn aside; the windows are open because of the heat, letting in the bubbling of the rain and the patter of chestnut leaves, still lushly green in the late spring. The streetlights paint the white ceiling amber.

If I'm to believe the brightly glowing alarm clock—which I do, a sometimes-trusting soul—the time approaches two in the morning.

"I just can't do it," Lyuba says and throws her pillow on the floor, stirring but not dislodging our family cat, who is purring with gusto. "I tried all kinds of positions. I counted sheep. I did breathing exercises. Nothing is working. I can't fall asleep. As soon as I close my eyes, I see my patients. I feel guilty to sleep when they suffer."

I try, but not very hard, to surface back to reality while dreams tug at my feet. I mumble, "The night is young."

"But I'm old."

I raise my head from my pillow. "You're thirty-four, baby," I say.

"I feel ancient. When you see so much pain every day, it sticks to you . . . Tell me a story. You have such a soothing voice."

"Come on," I say and close my eyes. "I have to go to work tomorrow. In by 7:30 AM. Out not earlier than 7:00 PM. Can't you prescribe yourself something? I've heard that barbiturates do wonders."

"Don't talk about things you don't understand. Tell me a story, or I'm calling the dream cops. And they will chop off your head."

"As you wish," I say. I have to tell her something light and easy. Something that weighs as light as a hair, carried by the wind. But nothing light comes to my mind. All my images are heavy, soaked by the night.

"OK," I say. "Just close your eyes, and don't open until I'm done."

"But it better be a good story. Or off with your head."

And I begin in dreamy monotone:

She was born from black earth, dry autumn leaves and a descending white cloud. She was playful in her childhood, as most of us are, but even in play, she was as graceful as well-bred royalty. Growing up, she spent summers gazing at meaty birds singing songs of procreation in the overgrown backyard, and at squirrels sprinting in the spruces. She spent winter days on a velvety blue couch, drinking the warm air with the entire surface of her body. She spent springs playing with friends on the front lawn or fighting enemies on the border of her property. Autumn was the best time. She lay on her back in dry leaves, watching the clouds, white as her belly, pass by.

Now, wearing a mantle of years, she counts twenty-four dreamy hours to a day, four seasons to a year. If she could talk, she would utter: "Happiness is only in your head." And her head has enough room for half of all the happiness in the world, and her belly has enough room for many mouthfuls of canned cuisine. And when she dies one fall, if ever, after living through many of them, children will place her furry, feline body in a shoe box and bury it in black earth, under dry autumn leaves, below an ascending white cloud.

I stop, and listen to Lyuba's even breath for a few moments. The rain ends. The streetlights continue their painting until the sun comes out.

The next night, when the alarm shows 1:30, she speaks again. "Tell me a story, please."

I awake and rub my eyes. "I don't know any more stories, honey. I'm sleepy. Give me a break."

A few hours before, we played cards. No Scrabble this, time, Lyuba said. I'm too tired.

The loser was supposed to take off an item of clothing. We both ended up in our underwear.

"You cheated," she said. "You took advantage of a tired woman. Next time we'll play Scrabble again." From the floor, she picked up her stockings, dress, belt, shoes, gloves, raincoat, beret, barrettes, bracelets and a Venetian mask in the shape of an eagle's head. The more you have on, the better are your chances. Lyuba is a practical woman. On the other hand, I started with shorts and a T-shirt.

"Guilty as charged, your Honor," I said. "I cheated so I could admire your breasts. But you're still a better player as is evident by your courageous resistance under unfair circumstances."

"You don't want me to call the dream cops, do you?" she says now.

"OK," I say. "This is the last time, though."

"It depends on the story. Last time it was too down to earth and too sad. I want something more abstract. Something amusing. A flight of fancy. Something that has no relationship to the real world, but is grounded in it. Are you up to the task?"

Isn't that what my life is? Amusing and unreal and full of responsibilities?

"Always," I say.

And I begin in a dreamy monotone:

He had a poker face only a mother could love—rectangular, perfectly flat, framed by flaming red hair, with a button nose, and with eyes so blue that they seemed to have splinters of the sky in the irises—a face as ungainly as a mixed metaphor, a face best described in the one-step-away-from-reality words of Nikolai Gogol.

She met his gaze with eyes of the same intense color. Their knees did not quite touch under the table. A single light above their heads let the rest of the room drown in the shadows.

She dropped her cards on the table for him to see. Four queens. He had seen her slip in the fourth queen—the queen of diamonds—but he didn't allow himself even the tiniest of smiles.

"Four kings," he said, holding his cards in front of her like the fan of a flamenco dancer.

She took a smoldering cigar from an ashtray shaped like a screaming mouth and puffed at it. She placed it back. She got up; sidewise she was as thin as the page of a book. Her diamond-studded earrings jingled.

She leaned toward him, letting him peek into the space where her breasts cleaved, and touched his hand. He withdrew it. Blood oozed from the place she touched—a paper cut.

"You're a cheater, your Highness," she said, and her voice caressed him like a peacock feather. "I hate you."

She turned away from him. From the back of her hat down to the bottom of her floor-length dress she was a complicated geometric pattern of two primary colors.

When she left, he pulled a handful of gold coins toward him, each stamped with words in a tongue no one speaks anymore, then took her cigar and sucked on it. Another king of hearts slipped from his sleeve and landed on the top of her discarded queens. He longed to kiss the paper-white skin of her neck. He knew she would come back. That was a rule of the game; they are a matching pair after all. The problem with her was that she always followed the rules. Even the bent ones.

He could live with that.

Lyuba's sleeping. I get up and draw the shades closed. My hands shake. It isn't hot any longer. Yawning, I return to bed. I close my eyes. Sleep will come. I'll just count a few sheep. A few fat, white, woolly, boring sheep, walking around me in circles. It will surely work. A sure thing. Just a few more moments. Sleep will come, and I'll sink under the surface of dreams, with my eyes closed, headfirst. Why should I think about the next night? If my storytelling skills fail me—but they won't—there are always barbiturates. With this amusing and unreal thought, I fall asleep.

House

It's 1989. I am thirty-nine.

"We'll buy this house," I tell my four-year-old Rachel who hangs onto my hand as if we are on a plane during a thunderstorm. She used to call me "mommy" because my wife was (and still is) always busy at work. She used to call my wife "baby," mimicking the way my wife addressed her.

The house is huge. It's a mansion, castle, palace. It's 232 square meters, which is 2500 square feet in the native tongue. Both my daughters will get their own bedrooms. I'll get an office, and there is a yard for the kids to play in. We can get another cat. When the rest of the family visits, we can accommodate them easily.

I'm afraid we won't be able to afford the house, but my wife is confident. "We both work, don't we?" she says.

Rachel is raising her accusatory eyes to me, as if saying, "Why are you lying to a little girl?"

"How will we take this house to our apartment?" she asks in her stilted Russian.

As we're moving in, a dark-skinned man approaches and shakes my hand.

"I'm Dr. Virumi," he says. "Are you a doctor?"

"My wife is," I say. I wish I could say that I'm at least a PhD, but I only have a master's degree. My wife is an internist, the first line of defense against diseases, after your own immune system. She's like a general, coordinating the fight, while specialists treat individual illnesses. She works for seventy-two hours straight, and still comes home cheerful. I can barely manage nine or ten. She's a superwoman and I am a wuss.

"This is a physician's ghetto," Dr. Virumi says. "Only doctors and their families live here. Except for Mr. Simpson over there. He's a malpractice lawyer."

At night, I can hear a dog barking at Mr. Simpson's house. I learn that the dog's name is Dogzilla, that she is a collie, and that she barks every night because she has phobias. I was told that Mr. Simpson took her to a special vet clinic in Syracuse, but nothing helps.

"You already forgot the half-wit from upstairs back home in Moldova," Lyuba says. We don't play Scrabble anymore. She's too busy.

A week later, I see Mr. Simpson in his driveway and go to shake his hand. His handshake is medium-firm. He's about my age, weight and height. If I were born in America, I could have been his spitting image. He gives me a million-dollar smile, gratis. Dogzilla barks at me from behind the fence. She probably fears that, like a Russian grizzly bear, I'll maul Mr. Simpson.

"Are you also a doctor?" he asks.

"My wife is," I say. "I hate to complain, Mr. Simpson, but can't something be done about Dogzilla's barking? I've heard they sell special collars for that."

His million-dollar smile self-destructs. "I don't feel that it's a problem. Let dogs be dogs," he says. Next time I pass by, he makes it a point to ignore me. I wave; there's no response. My heart pounds hard when he does that.

A couple of months later, I fly to a conference to present my paper entitled "Zero insertion force compliant pin contact and assembly." The plane gets into a thunderstorm when we approach Florida. I miss holding Rachel's hand.

In the conference hall, I climb on the podium, armed with a collapsible pointer. It could also be used as a weapon to strike an attacking dog. It's ninety degrees outside, but indoors it's chilly like a morgue. I turn on the slide projector and dim the lights. The hall is full, but I've gotten the worst time for the presentation—right after the lunch break. I adjust my tie and cough loudly. A corpse in the front row opens one eye and closes it again. He's clearly not interested in zero insertion forces.

I put up a slide with a blood-red background, extracting a loud "Oh" from the part of the audience that still has a spark of consciousness in them. They are not used to creative coloring. The corpse and most of his brethren come back to life. I smile. Now, when I have their attention, all I need to do is to sustain it. This is much easier. When I'm done, they clap. The former corpse in the front row shakes my hand and gives me his business card. His hand feels like a slice of salmon refrigerated for days.

When I get back to the hotel, I call home.

"We had a freak snow storm," Lyuba says. "My car got stuck. Guess who helped me push it out?"

"Santa Claus?"

"Mr. Simpson."

I turn off the lights and slide into a creaky bed. A TV sings behind the thin wall. Sleeping is out of the question. Jewish sages say that shame is the greatest punishment. My cheeks are red as if I was slapped repeatedly.

When I return home, I buy a bag of sugar bones for Dogzilla. I ring Mr. Simpson's doorbell. There are seven SUVs parked in his driveway. He comes out and eyes me as if I am a Russian grizzly bear. I hand him bones. He puts his hands behind his back.

"Thanks, but no thanks," he says.

At night, I can hear Dogzilla's barking. She's not happy. My wife sleeps soundlessly as if my younger daughter is right and she is really a baby. What am I to do? Join Dogzilla and howl at the moon? I need Mr. Simpson's permission for that, but he would probably say that he feels it is a problem. Finally, my eyes close, and the house embraces me in its American dream.

Yankee Husband

Came to Town

It's 1990. I am forty. I slouch in my chair at my Uncle Grisha's party, tasting the headache that grows fast behind my forehead like one of those bone-colored mushrooms in my front yard. Technically, he is my wife's uncle, but we share everything. As they say in Russian, "The husband and wife are the same devil." Actually, my wife is an angel.

It's Uncle Grisha's sixtieth. In time-honored medieval fashion, the guests surround the table according to their rank. They are mostly Uncle Grisha and Aunt Manya's friends from New York City, all in their late fifties and early sixties, all immigrants. Most of them came from the famous city of Odessa, the birthplace of most Russian comedians. Aunt Manya directs the more important people closer to Uncle Grisha and herself, and the Russian visitors—to the far end. It's like in a full bus. The newcomers get the worst seats or are forced to stand. The visitors are my wife's sister and nephew. They are my sister and nephew now.

The table is long and rests on two carved lion paws, taken from an exotic wooden lion hunted down in Shanghai or Mexico City. The other two paws are employed by a bureau in the next room. The table is covered by a cloth as white as an angel's robe. A clear plastic sheet over the cloth protects it from the elements. The dining room smells of Aunt Manya's *piroshki*, Smirnoff, Manishevitz, cognac, perfume, roses and faintly of sweat.

We had plenty of sweat back home, buckets of it, but as for the rest, it took some effort to acquire it. Hungry homemakers equipped with string bags we called "maybe" would accumulate at dawn by the closed grocery store doors. At first, they elbowed each other silently. Then, they would start cursing in Russian, Moldovan, Ukrainian and Yiddish. When the line reached the critical mass, it smashed the doors with the bodies of the old ladies who came even earlier, and now had the misfortune to be at the head of the line. Then, the homemakers would surge forward like salmon upstream, while the fallen but resilient old ladies bit their ankles and thighs. Cops with complicated geometrical patterns on their shoulder boards blew their whistles. And all this for a blue, cadaverous chicken, sausage with more garlic than meat, a small raisin roll called "caloric bun" and bread, dark like the thoughts of a desperate man. If Bulgarian jam or Chinese canned pork appeared thanks to a distribution error, the mob would overwhelm the cops and riot to their hearts content.

When Lyuba shopped, she was easily outflanked, outmaneuvered and outgunned. I arrived as the reinforcement, but by that time the shelves carried only a few glass jars of pickled beets, a sack or two of grief-striken potatoes and maybe some moldy flower rejected by rodents. I would shake my fist at the plump saleswomen who stood grinning behind the safety of the wide marble counters, but my wife would embrace me and then lead us away. And beets would never taste so good ever again.

At Grisha's table everything is civilized. No biting, smashing or fist shaking. Music, recorded at the restaurant "Odessa," booms in the language of Lev Nikolayevich Tolstoy, Anton Pavlovich Chekhov, Osip Emilevich Mandelshtam and Mikhail Sergeyevich Gorbachev. I sit almost at the end of the table, one hierarchical notch above the Russian guests, discreetly peeking into *The New Yorker* magazine in my lap. I'm entitled to a better seat, but gave it up. Not that I'm against ranking. Just that sometimes a man exchanges honor and privilege for the quiet life of a country bumpkin. That's American-style freedom.

"On escho mozhet!" one of the Uncle's friends says, pointing to Uncle Grisha. "He still can! Maybe even twice a night!"

Like everyone else, he's speaking Russian, of course. The friend is dressed in a green silk shirt, unbuttoned almost to his navel. Its front bears a fresh mayonnaise stain. He's a wooly mammoth under the shirt.

"*Emu ne nado pomoch*," Aunt Manya says. She wears a brooch the size of a baby's head attached to her lilac gown above the place where her breasts used to entice. "He needs no help. He gets it up all by himself!"

My wife says nothing though I know she doesn't like this type of talk. Her sister . . . my sister . . . the sister is also silent. Her son, a boy of fourteen, sits next to me. When I was his age, I would kill for his traveling freedom and access to a table like this. Maybe not quite killed, but maimed. Figuratively speaking. And only the people who were responsible for limiting my travel and diet, naturally. But he, he gets it all without maiming. That's progress, which I like, speaking in general terms.

"Will we go to Manhattan tomorrow, Uncle?" he asks. "I want to see the Statue of Liberty."

"Good choice," I say loudly. "Liberty and justice for all. Let's drink to progress."

The woman next to me gives me the evil eye. She seems like she has plenty of them to give.

"Grisha is a tiger," she says, turning away, and peeling the skin from her chicken with two forks. "Our very own Stallonnie," pronouncing Stallone with the "e" on the end.

The green-shirt man makes an obscene gesture as if by mistake, and his wife slaps him. Everybody laughs. They are so funny. A bunch of stand-up comedians. Only they sit while performing, and it's free. Am I lucky or what?

Nobody dares poke fun at Aunt Manya, at least not directly. She's the boss in her small Manhattan Laundromat, and governs her two employees, Uncle Grisha included, with an iron jabbing finger and a voice as loud as a jet at takeoff.

"*Hvatit!*" Aunt Manya says. "Enough! Let's talk about something intellectual . . . I'm sick and tired of this so-called cultural Manhattan. I don't understand what highbrows find there. You should've seen that culture! People are urinating in the streets in broad daylight! You know what I would do if I were the mayor of New York? I would tell the cops to pick them all up, drive them Upstate into the sticks, tie them to a tree, and let them urinate there until a bear bites off their pricks."

"That's why you're not the mayor," Uncle Grisha says and laughs, displaying his high-quality American teeth. His Russian teeth—steel, silver, and gold—are gone, like leaves in the fall.

The guests laugh, too. Except for my household.

"Isn't she funny?" Uncle Grisha asks me, coming all the way down to me and jabbing my ribs with his elbow that feels as if made of granite.

"Unbelievably funny," I say. I want to crawl outside and howl at the American moon. It's not full for nothing. On the other hand, it looks like a very pale beet.

"Hey, big guy, do you despise us, you Yankee?" Uncle Grisha asks. He puts almost as much venom in the word "Yankee" as the Moscow demonstrators did when they shouted, "Yankee go home" back during the Vietnam War.

"Just because you made it in America and we didn't?" he presses on. "And why did you grow a beard like a religious Jew?"

"I don't despise you, Uncle Grisha," I say. "I'm a little tired. It's been a long drive. And not only religious Jews grow beards. Lenin had a beard. He wasn't a religious Jew. Yasir Arafat has a beard. He wasn't—"

"Bullshit. It's only four hours."

"Yes, but I'm not used to the city traffic."

The four of us—my wife, sister, nephew, and I—sleep in the basement. Though it's finished, it has no windows. There isn't much room in the house because Uncle and Aunt are renting out the second floor. Real estate is expensive in New York. Good thing our kids are home with the babysitter.

I'm claustrophobic. The fan is off because it's too cold for the women. The nightlight ogles me from the corner with its single ruby eye. I wish I could toss and turn, but I'm afraid to wake up my wife. I can hear my nephew tossing and turning.

The next morning, we drive to Lower Manhattan. When you drive in the City during the day, is it a daymare? I park our Saab (I hate it because it's less reliable than a burning match in the wind) in the garage and walk behind my family to Battery Park. We take pictures. The Russian guests with Lady Liberty in the background. The Russian guests with the Manhattan skyline in the background. My wife with the Russian guests. The Russian guests and me. All of us together (taken by a respectable-looking Japanese tourist, but I probably still look apprehensive in the shot because I took some great memories with this camera and what if he'd run away with it?).

The guests are dressed in American clothes; my wife loses no time in throwing them into the melting pot. They still don't look like Americans. None of us does.

A homeless man urinates on a tree. The dry leaves in his beard are color-coordinated with his yellow hair. Very picturesque. He sings, "Yankee Doodle came to town." He's probably a patriot and a history buff. He does look like a native.

We board the ferry. I stand next to my nephew. The Manhattan skyline is as breathtaking as a fist in the solar plexus. I wish my brother could stand here as well. I would tell him jokes I can't say in front of my nephew. My brother is not a refusnik any longer since the Russian pharaohs are gone, but now the American government refuses to give him the entry visa. That's the funniest joke of them all. We are sending him jeans and leather jackets, of course. That's the least we can do.

"Do you like it in America?" I ask the boy. "Maybe you'll come here to study in a few years? Our colleges are top-notch."

I have no first-hand experience with "our colleges," but everyone knows that they are top-notch. So I let the boy know this, too, in case he hasn't heard it yet.

"I like Russia," he says. "It's my home."

His eyes are huge. Did I have eyes like that when I was his age? What kind of person was I then? Smart—check. Handsome—check. Original— you bet. I sigh. When I try to look back, it's like gazing through consecutive layers of glass. Each is clear, but when you have them piled up, the distance looks distorted. Add to that a few emotions of various colors and thickness, and the picture is not pretty anymore, assuming it ever was.

"Millions of people left their homes to come here," I say. That's the argument I use with my wife all the time, so it drops easily from my lips. "This is the land of opportunity. See this bronze lady up there? The tall, green one? She beckons you."

My nephew is a bit green as well. He's getting seasick though the waters are calm.

We land and snap more pictures. We eat hotdogs and French fries. We drink Coke. We listen to patriotic music. We sit on the bench and stare at the passersby and the green lady.

"You can do what you want here," I tell my nephew. "Travel. Vote. Make money. Be happy. That's what America is all about. The land of freedom and prosperity. In Russia, you're gloomy and oppressed. Don't tell me it's not true. I've been there. It's a colossus—"

"We came here, didn't we? And please, please, Uncle, don't call my country a colossus with feet of clay. That would be too mean."

"I would never say something like that, boy. And as for your coming here, how long did it take to secure the paperwork? And they let you come only because your father and brother stay behind as hostages. Very medieval."

If I ever was original, it looks like I've lost my touch.

We drive back to Brooklyn. My nephew sits next to me while Lyuba and her sister chat in the back.

"See," I say. "Uncle Grisha and Aunt Manya have a house. We have a house. But the four of you live in a one-room apartment. That's the ugly side of Socialism."

A car full of teenagers cuts me off. The driver, a girl with the flamboyant red hair of a Dante Gabriel Rossetti painting, flips me a birdie. She mouths something that probably has nothing to do with my ability to reflect on politics. I'm lucky she doesn't shoot.

"Gorbachev is a reformist," the boy says. "We'll be as good as you economically. We are better than you socially because our country takes care of its people."

Wow. Is he really fourteen?

The Dante girl took the exit. I'm safe for the next few moments.

"Mark my words, boy," I say. "The Soviet Union will collapse soon. And then things will get ugly."

"Never, Uncle. We are the indestructible union of free republics put together by great Russia."

I sigh. He's quoting verbatim from the national anthem of the USSR. It seems like the boy took after his father Piotr, that demagogue. We enter Brooklyn. I park by Uncle Grisha's house. Kids, yelling in Spanish, play basketball across the street. I look forward to a leftover dinner, to the friendly conversation with my extended family and to another night in the Uncle's basement.

The following day, we drive Upstate. It takes us four hours as always. Four hours of fun and stimulating conversations. I park my hated Saab by our new house where mushrooms grow silently, turn to my wife, and lie: "We are home, honey."

The next day, Annie calls to tell us that her father has died. I fly to the funeral. Lyuba is too busy at work. My brother and parents don't come either. I don't approach Annie except for a very brief hug. She looks great; my wife looks great as well. They just don't age like other women do.

I feel that I will explode unless I talk to her, but she is always surrounded by people. I spent several hours in the park across from her house. She's my girlfriend now, though we have never been intimate, not even in words. Doesn't matter. I know what she feels, and that's enough for me. I don't need to do the statistical analysis of her words to make sure it's true.

When I get home, and Lyuba embraces me, I enjoy her warmth.

I digitize Annie's photograph so I can have her in front of me while I'm working. My wife never gets at my computer, and as for the kids, I keep Annie's image in the same folder as those of all relatives, including Uncle Michael. I'm Bond. James Bond.

I wish my father had a computer like that back in the sixties. He has never received his PhD. It's hard to do statistical analysis without a computer. But you still can love someone, even if you cook on a coal-fired stove or write with a quill.

The Rich and the Poor

It's 1991. I am forty-one.

The Soviet Union is collapsing, and the sound of its fall reverberates all over the world. It makes a splash like that great tree falling into that great ocean in the nursery rhyme "If All the Seas Were One Sea." The Bolsheviks are turning in their graves like spinning CDs. Lenin probably drops a furtive tear when no one is watching. I am driving my family to New York City while listening to NPR. A caller rumbles something about Russian air force. The anchor stops him. "Russia has no air force," she says.

The caller stumbles. He's probably a typical American. To him, the Soviet Union *is* Russia. But soon, the seventy-year confusion will end. There will be no Soviet Union. There will be a Russian air force, Russian nukes, Russian crime, and even a Russian president. I hope they will throw Lenin out of the Mausoleum and turn it into a museum honoring the victims of the Soviet state.

I thought it wouldn't happen in my lifetime, clay feet notwithstanding.

"Why are the Russians so poor?" Mila asks. She is fifteen now, and her sister, Rachel, is seven.

"Not all of them are," I say. "Some Russians are middle class. Take us, for example. We are not rich, but can be considered well-off."

My wife and Rachel play with a coloring book in the back. I can see them in the mirror.

"Yeah, but remember how dirty the bathroom was in that Russian-American restaurant we went to last year?"

I don't, but I have to show that daddies remember everything. Home-grown authorities shouldn't be challenged needlessly.

"American restaurant bathrooms can be dirty also," I say. "Nothing is clean about this important business."

"No way. They're clean."

She's either patriotic or the women's bathrooms are cleaner that the men's. Maybe American women are more into hygiene than American men, and they wash their hands after they go to the bathroom for all I know.

I accelerate. The relatively clean and pothole-free Route 380 rolls under the tires of my car. American road, Japanese car, Russian driver, Italian opera coming from the radio—Karl Marx would approve of this display of international solidarity.

"Even if they are clean," I say, "there are other things by which you can judge the nation's prosperity other than the cleanness of its bathrooms."

"It's easy for you to say. You don't have to sit on those seats all the time."

This is true. I've never taken a seat in the stall of a Russian-American restaurant, though I might have my chance tonight. But I need to change the subject. I know that kids like scatological humor, but a good father should steer the conversation into something more educational. I want to be a good father. Not an excellent one, because that's too much work for too little difference. The law of diminishing returns in action. Let everyone say that I have a heart of silver instead of gold, and that's enough compliment for me. Silver is also precious and handy. I have both gold and silver crowns, and I can't tell the difference when I explore them with my tongue.

Moreover, some daddies have a heart of bronze or even stone. To be in the upper strata of daddy universe is not a bad thing.

"This restaurant will be different," I say. "The other one was just a little eatery. This one is the real thing. You'll see, and I promise you will enjoy it. It's very classy. A fine example of a Russian-Jewish-American institution. Do you know what institution means?"

She glares at me. Oops. Of course she knows what institution means. She has a great vocabulary. I am getting too forgetful for a man with a heart of silver. I guess I'm reaching my silver years.

Insomniacs are always hungry. Maybe that explains why New York, the city that never sleeps, always eats. While we sleep well in Rienville, we get the eating bug every time we come down to the City. Combine that with the educational experience for the kids, and you get something that can only happen in this place of hybrid cultures.

As soon as we park our Saab and approach the restaurant, a fine example of a Russian-Jewish-American institution, the exotica hits our faces like a cloud of exhaust from a garbage truck. Two longhaired beings of an undetermined sex, in leather jackets and crew cuts, flank the doors. Lit cigarettes dangle from their thin lips. If the eyes are the mirrors of the soul, their souls are dingy rooms filled with drug paraphernalia and assault weapons. Both emanate alcohol-saturated fumes. I'm afraid they would demand protection money, called "the roof" in Russian, for the privilege to enter, but they let us go without a word.

Once we are seated by the match-thin hostess in a leather skirt and white blouse with puffy sleeves, we order *komplexniy obed* rather than à la carte, to get the whole gamut of experience.

It's like a tsar's banquet from a history book, except that no tsar would ever invite so many Jews.

The waiter keeps bringing and bringing stuff and not giving us any reprieve. Slices of paper-thin fish shaped like a petal, arranged in an open-flower pattern, herring in sour cream sauce, a green salad sprinkled with goat cheese, broiled lamb and chicken on a bed of rice, three types of sushi, potato salad, beef tongue, pickled cucumber, and watermelon, white fish, clams on a bed of noodles and, of course, the mandatory blini with red caviar. And the drinks: seltzer water from the Caucasian mountains, wine and vodka. For dessert: a chocolate cake and three different pastries. The waiter brings new dishes, piling the new ones on top of the others because there is no room left on the table.

My wife quit eating first, followed by Rachel and then Mila. They only return to nibbling at the arrival of the dessert. I keep consuming dutifully until the end. I finish off each plate because it's all paid for and it tastes good.

The patrons at the surrounding tables keep up with their portions. Somehow most find time to smoke a cigarette or two between the dishes and make plenty of loud toasts.

The band arrives after eight o'clock. It consists of only two players singing PG-rated songs. A young woman with a tambourine wears a long, plastic raincoat, a short skirt and Cleopatra wig; and a googly-eyed, round-faced man fast approaching middle age, plays an electric guitar. They vocalize mostly in Russian, and in an un-close approximation of different European languages. The patrons dance to their music, elbowing each other on the tiny dance floor, smoldering cigarettes in their flailing hands.

Time for the bathroom trip. I hope it's clean. Inside, it's richly decorated with fake marble. There is enough chrome here for a whole fleet of bikes. An unsteady man leans toward the urinal. Though heavily bearded, he doesn't look either Jewish or Russian. First of all, he wears faded jeans, a checkered shirt, and cowboy boots—a stark contrast to the dressed up guests. Second, he beams that friendly American grin. Maybe he's the janitor.

"Howdy, hon," he says, zipping up. I can smell vodka on his breath.

"Howdy." I'm sure I sound like a Texan. The kind who spent his formative years in Siberia.

He winks and gestures toward the stall. I don't know what he's trying to say, so I just nod and proceed with my business at the urinal. He watches me as if he's never seen a grown man pee. Then he opens the door to the stall, gets inside and beckons me with his curled finger. Maybe he's a plumber. I give him a wide American grin. If he thinks that I understand the cowboy bathroom lingo, he is mistaken.

I turn to leave.

"Fuck you, man," he yells.

I know that I failed him, but don't know how.

Back in the dining area, the belly dancers churn for the sake of the older crowd, upping the ratings to PG-13.

Our daughters say "gross," and turn away. So does my wife. She says that she regrets coming here. She says that it's the last time we take a trip like this. She didn't know about the belly dancers and that the *komplexniy obed* included so much alcohol. She didn't know that the tobacco smoke would be so dense.

I suggest that we leave right away, but she says that since this is the last time, we should persevere until the end. I say that this is the end. She says that we should dance. So we do. My wife says that the dancing was the best part of the evening though I'm a terrible dancer. The kids say that our dancing was gross.

Outside, not a single star shines in a sky the color of asphalt. Someone scratched our car with something sharp. I hope they used keys instead of knives.

"Is this how they party in Russia?" Mila asks.

I want to say that this was a unique experience, a mixture of three cultures that produces something totally different, but Lyuba pre-empts me.

"This was ugly," she says. "A parody produced by a fat, lazy mind."

"I'm not coming here again. Ever," Mila says.

"Me too," Rachel agrees. I sigh with relief. If they agree with each other, maybe there will be no battle on the way back.

"Was the bathroom clean here?" I ask Mila. "Ours was very lavishly decorated. They even have an attendant to give you fresh towels. Shows you clearly that not all Russians are poor."

"Whatever," she says.

I feel acid rise in my chest. "Anybody want a hamburger and a Coke?" I ask. Family is above all for me. Maybe I do have a heart of gold.

To Own the Block

IT'S 1994. I am forty-four. Rachel—she is eight now—plays on the piano, and Mura sings on the bench next to her, her fangs glistening as she opens her mouth for another note. Rachel recently grew tall enough to reach the pedals, and she's happy.

I watch Rachel from my chair, with a half smile on my face that gets heavier every year. My lap is full of Mura's hair, black, white and brown. Earlier today, I got a $2000 a year raise. According to my boss, that's a lot for an engineer of my performance. Last year my raise was zero. My performance is good, but who am I to argue? I'm only a small cogwheel in the company's machine, and in today's economy, it's cheaper to replace it when it squeaks than to grease it.

Lyuba bursts into the room, her cheeks flaming. She's normally very composed, but when she is protecting her offspring, she is a large panther, with a twitching tail and ears flat against her head. I get up from the sofa to preempt the lunge. My knees creak.

"You know, dear, I just read a story about a man who owned Vermont. He just drove there after a fight with his wife, and when he came back, he gave Vermont to her as a present. They've never fought again. I walked around the next block down the street this morning and want to give it to you, darling."

"Stop talking nonsense," she says. Her eyes are like emeralds I saw catching sun in a Tiffany's window. "Don't you see that Mura's breaking the child's concentration? Get her out of here!"

"They both distract me, Mommy," the child says without turning. "They don't care how I will do on the recital. They need grounding."

I pick up the cat and carry her outside. She's heavy, almost twenty pounds. I ease her onto the warm asphalt of the driveway. Spring waves at me with a young poplar's branches.

"We need to lose weight, Mura. Both of us."

Mura rubs her head against my knee and sings in her melodic voice. Another half a dozen hairs stick to the pant leg of my Dockers.

"Would you like to own the block, Mura? Suppose there is no law against that?"

Mura lies down and tucks her front paws under her chest.

"They keep raising taxes on the house every year," I continue. "Unless you own a McMansion, they squeeze you for what you're worth and more. Why can't renters like you pay school taxes? Some renters are wealthy. You, for example, own a pet carrier, a litter box, a rug and a kitty house. There ought to be a law. I'll tell you what. If you agree to be the legal owner, I'll feed you tuna fish every day. Tempting, isn't it?"

She gets up, raises her tail and walks away, suddenly unattainable like a model in a sable coat. I watch her disappearing into the bushes. I sigh. I might need an evening job.

Cat's Magic

It's 1998. I am forty-eight. A middle-aged man who's afraid of cold weather. What's next? Winters in Florida? Battery-heated socks? AARP?

When I get to be fifty, it's not just going down the hill. It means no one will hire me should I lose my job. Being fifty is like leprosy in the ancient world. They treat you as if you are an empty cask without feelings or soul.

Daisy washes her face under a naked maple tree. Her paw moves over her ear and across her cheek with the smooth precision of a master make-up artist. She is ready to meet Mr. Tom right now, despite the late season. She was born to be timid, but threw off the bonds of domestic oppression, including the flea collar, by the force of her personality. She was certainly a goddess a few lives ago, and her worshippers scratched behind her ear and sacrificed cheese, tuna fish and bologna in her honor.

The last leaf falls from the tree, touching her shoulder, startling her for a moment. She brushes it off, gets up and rubs her head against my pant leg, leaving a few white and black hairs on it. The colors of the day and the colors of the night. Any philosopher would hire her for inspiration.

A few minutes later, Daisy and a ginger cat from across the street yell, spit and hiss at each other on my lawn. It's the battle of the superpowers, and block dominance is at stake. Daisy wins and runs after the ginger to finish her off.

I take a few hairs from my pant leg, throw them up and wish for spring. The wind blows them away; a few moments later the first snowflake lands on my palm. It melts instantly. Surely, spring is coming, as if by magic. And I will be young and hot-blooded again. And my brother and his family will finally get their American visas. All in exchange for the occasional ear scratching and a few cans of tuna fish. I struck a great bargain, and I still get to keep my soul.

Talking about the soul. Talking about the body. Talking about love.

"I'm studying Kabbalah," Annie tells me. "We talked about *bashert*— the soul mate. Barry and I are *basherts*."

I'm stunned. She's clearly mistaken. I'm her *bashert*. She doesn't need some stinking Barry. I knew her before he did. Not in the Biblical sense, not carnal or anything but still . . .

"Is Barry studying it, too?" I ask carefully.

"No, he's too busy."

This is the answer, then. I have to study Kabbalah so I will get an edge over Barry, and follow Annie into the world to come instead of him. Unlike my other good intentions that never move beyond the planning stage, I act on this one. My wife joins me, and we take classes together, like a good couple should. I learn that people can have several *basherts*. I love Lyuba and feel so guilty about the entire affair—though I'm guiltless on the surface—that I have nightmares as regularly as a young, healthy woman's menses. Does it mean I have two *basherts*, like Biblical Jacob did—Rachel and Leah? But American laws frown upon polygamy. I suspect that both Annie and my wife would, too. I don't even want to think about the kids. The Biblical heroes had it easier in some ways. I need to learn more, so I sign up for another Kabbalah course.

The Patent Game

It's 1999. I am forty-nine.

Unlike most humans, the patent lawyer doesn't like food—except sugarless gum. Even before he told me about his tastes, I guessed that. He looks like a skeleton that just emerged from someone's closet after spending years in the company of old suits, shirts with yellow stains under the armpits, ties that lost their power and eternal moths.

I came to fight him, but he doesn't know it yet.

The lawyer doesn't smell of anything, as if he's already beyond decay. He smiles with his lipless mouth. His ears are the only fleshy part of his body, at least from among the visible parts. Something, and it can't be his eyes, glistens in his eye sockets. His bony fingers flip the pages. At least he doesn't wet them with saliva. I'm grateful for that.

Unlike me, the lawyer is not a HAL employee, but a contractor. This way, the company can avoid paying him benefits. They probably searched hard under rocks for the cheapest one.

I'm here to discuss my new invention so he can file it with the Patent Office. I invented a way to add a new dimension of senses to multimedia—the sense of smell. "Invented" is too strong of a word. "Everything that can be invented has already been invented." That's what Charles Duell, Commissioner of the United States Patent Office, apparently said back in 1899. I only perfected what someone else has done. And that someone else perfected the invention of his predecessor. I don't stand on the shoulders of a giant. I stand on the shoulders of a pigmy like me. The giant is way below, at the bottom of the pyramid of pigmies. He must be very patient, like Atlas.

"We should write the clauses as broad as possible," the lawyer says. His voice is pleasant.

I nod. I don't need another pigmy on my shoulders.

"Gum?" he offers. The gum smells of watermelon. I overate watermelons when I was a child, and I have hated them ever since. I refuse.

"And yet they should be concrete and not watered-down," he continues. He doesn't chew on his.

I imagine a broad-shoulder man in concrete boots, ready to be dropped overboard by two sleazy types in pinstripe suits. I don't want to get watered-down, and I don't want my clauses to suffer either. I know exactly what I want. So I nod again.

"Let's start with the title," he says. "Method and apparatus for transmitting a parameter based on a plurality of carrier signals . . ."

He goes on in a pleasant monotone. I try to suppress a yawn but fail. He stops.

"Maybe we should reschedule?" he asks.

"No, no," I say. "Please go on. I'm all ears."

"In that case, let's discuss the Abstract."

Wow, all we did was the Title? I thought we were already on Claims. Eventually, after a few ice fields in Greenland melt, and a few billion lattes are consumed in New York City, we arrive to Claims. I wake up. Here's the moment I was waiting for.

"You can't have this claim," he says.

"Which one? You know that I'm an engineer, not a patent lawyer." I pretend that I'm an innocent bystander. I can pretend all I want. The fight is inevitable. We will lock horns.

"This claim: 'an aroma converter for encoding aroma information into standard electrical signals.'"

I'm still hoping I can get by. I'm trying to inoculate him with my naiveté. "And why not?"

"Because this claim is too broad."

"No, it's not. In 'Frank, Stein et al,' they had a claim as broad as this and even broader."

"Young man! Let me be the judge of that."

He has his own dark agenda. It's much more complicated than a chess game. I can only guess his motivations. Perhaps my invention is too revolutionary, and he's a reactionary. Perhaps he's envious of my creativity.

Perhaps HAL sets up some kind of bureaucratic limit on him. None of this makes any sense on the surface, but the rules of the corporate world are as twisted as mountain passes. All I know is that he wants to remove this clause, which is equivalent to a patent castration. If he wins, another inventor will easily circumvent this patent. He mustn't win. Since the easy way didn't get me anywhere, I have to play my trump card.

"Do you want to see the prototype model?" I ask.

He waves his finger. "Not really."

I take out the model from the briefcase and put it on his table. He stares at me. I press the button, and in a few seconds the room is filled with the scent of incense. It smells just like a Russian Orthodox church I visited once. Russians are great believers in evil forces, and try to frighten them away by all means, including smells.

"Do you like it?" I ask.

His fingers tremble. From what I know of the patent law, he doesn't like it.

"A prototype is not necessary for a patent application," he says. "Turn on the fan."

I pretend to press another button, but the fan that is supposed to clear the smell doesn't turn on. This fan is one of the top features of my invention. You have to remove the old smell if you want to get a new one started. Since it doesn't work, the incense aroma lingers. The lawyer gets up and tries to open the window. His nails scratch the latch, putting my teeth on edge. He probably forgot that we are in the basement, and the windows are only for decoration.

"Excuse me," he says. "I'll be right back."

He heads for the door, but I'm already there with a burning incense stick in my hand. This will be my tenth patent. I know how to handle his kind.

"What do you want?" he asks.

"I want this claim as written."

He returns to the table and gets his pen out. Is it really a gun? Will he shoot me with it as James Bond did?

"Turn on the fan," he says, "and I will do it."

I press the button again, for real this time, and the fan sucks out the aroma of the incense. We stare at each other's sleeves. What legal tricks are stored up there? He coughs. I force him back into the closet. In a few moments, he will announce his defeat. Any second now. I'm as good as a winner.

When the pause stretches out too much, like an overburdened bungee cord, I ask, "So?"

"So, what?"

I put my hand back on the button. "I thought we had an agreement."

He sighs, writes down the claim the way I want it, and hands the pen to me for my signature. I've won the match. I'm patent savvy.

Bonding

It's 1999. I am still forty-nine. Rachel reads my manuscript with the same stern look that I see on her mother when she talks to her patients on the phone. It doesn't matter if my manuscript is funny or not; reading is serious work. Outside, the neighbor's dog Phantom barks in a deep, operatic voice. He's recently neutered.

"Like it?" I ask. "'There is nothing sadder than a man who has to rely on his child's help' is my favorite line."

"It's dull . . . and uninspiring," Rachel says. She pushes the pages aside and glares at me through her glasses. Her vocabulary is great for a fifteen-year-old. I'm especially proud that she didn't say, "It's, like, boring."

I collect the pages and press them together with a paper clip. My fingers never tremble. That's the kind of man I am. As stern and emotionless as my father.

"Sorry to waste your time," I say.

"You need to study writing," she says, getting up and smoothing her skirt. "Instead, you play video games."

"Video games are not a waste of time," I say. "They help me be creative."

"Hah-hah-hah," she says. "Hah-hah-hah as in 'not funny.'"

"I do study, really. I can quote Mark Twain for you. He said, 'If you catch an adjective, kill it.' My take is that you can't catch them all. They are like ticks in the woods. Better just to avoid the places where they congregate."

"Whatever."

Yesterday, I read this line to my wife: "'She had a heart of gold, and that's why she did everything with a heavy heart.' Like it?"

She stops chopping up the carrots and turns to me. She wears an apron embroidered with the words "Hot Stuff." I like everything hot.

"Why are your female characters always negative?"

Are they? I just want to make them feminine. Is femininity negative?

"OK," I say aloud. "I get your point. How about, 'He had a heart of gold, and that's why he did everything with a heavy heart?' Better?"

"It's sick. By the way, have you given any more thought to a vasectomy?"

Now, I take my manuscript to the porch and read it to my cat, giving her a page to sniff beforehand, to stimulate her interest.

"You know that English is my second language, don't you?"

She has a look as if she wants to say, "If you think that I know this, why are you asking?" I squint my eyes, since I've read some place that it makes cats comfortable, but she still watches me suspiciously while I read. She doesn't even tuck in her front paws under her chest. I wish we had a writers group in town.

"Like it?" I say when I'm done. "This is my favorite line: 'nothing is funnier than a person reduced to the animal state.'"

She walks away without even raising her bushy tail. It's quite a tale. Am I funny or what?

Phantom is choking behind the fence. I approach him and clear my throat. He stops barking and cocks his bony head. I read out loudly.

"Like it?" I ask. "'You can stop worrying about your health as soon as you are dead.' That was my favorite line."

He whimpers. I didn't know he had such expressive eyes. I think he might be able to play video games if trained properly, or at least voice his approval when I get a high score. I go back to the house to get him a sugar bone, making sure my wife and daughter don't see me. They'd say that male bonding is so overrated. The genderless sun (grammatically speaking, it has the neutral gender in Russian) bakes my neck and the bald spot on the top of my head. There is nothing sadder than a man who has to rely on abstractions.

Ask Me a Question

It's 2000. I am fifty. My friend Albert never asks me, "How are you?" He answers my questions about his health, his kids, his house, his job, his finances, his girlfriend, his opinions, but he never asks about me. He seldom returns my phone calls. As for e-mail, just forget about it. Other than that, he's the friendliest man in the world. That's why I like him. I have no idea why he likes me. I wouldn't if I were him.

It's often difficult to talk to him. I've heard this saying before: "If you think everything is possible, try to nail jelly to a tree." But I can do that. Just give me enough nails.

I'm the only one who calls him Albert. Everyone else calls him Al. I say that Al is the chemical symbol for aluminum, and it's not a proper name. He laughs. He likes to laugh.

Like me, Albert is balding. Like me, he's an amateur writer. Like me, he loves to go to the movies, play pool and eat pizza. We get sick at the same time. Occasionally, I call him, leave a message and then call again and again, until I finally reach him. He works two jobs and is busy.

We usually go to the movies, and then to play pool (he always wins) and after that to the pizza place Brother Giuseppe's, where we eat the greasy, delicious dough smothered with cheese and tomato sauce and spices—*cucina Italiana, vera cucina,* as Albert says—while he corrects my stories' grammar. He pats his slices with a napkin to remove excess oil. I don't. He exercises regularly. I don't. I envy his will power.

Our mutual friend Nelson asks me questions about my life all the time, but he gives me only thirty seconds to answer. Then it's his turn to talk about what interests him. And for that, there is no stop or inter-ruption. Not that I want him to stop. He talks about literature, politics and religion, the subjects I love. That's why he's my friend. Besides, I can feed people a lot of information in thirty seconds.

When all three of us meet it must look hilarious to outsiders. Fortu-nately, outsiders are not very curious at these longitudes. People here are busy and practical, and have no time for nonsense. If Captain Cook or Dr. Livingston had landed here instead of their final destinations, no one would have given them a second glance, let alone ate them or asked presumptuous questions.

We go to Barnes and Noble to pick up a dozen books and magazines and sit around a table at the cafe, eating pastries.

Nelson says something like this: "I'm not sure if God exists. If He does, why does he allow all the cruelty in the world?"

I say something like this: "I have a theory of everything. God designed the Universe, but his logic is not human. Therefore, we can't understand it. It seems illogical to us but in reality, it's perfect. We just can't see its perfection from our limited viewpoint."

Albert says something like this: "My neighbor has a white plastic statue of a man holding a Bible in his front yard. He probably thinks that God exists. I have a Madonna figurine on my night table. It makes the view from my bed somewhat limited."

This time, Nelson is not with us. Earlier today, Albert and I watched a horror movie, "The Last Stand of the Body Pluckers." Something about dream invasions by aliens from outer space, a subject that is particularly frightening to both of us. Next time, we should check the movie subject before we go. Now, after three games of pool (Albert won all three), we are at a buffet for a change—all you can eat, including drinks and dessert.

The buffet is also frightening, with so many people who are as wide as they are tall. Men are dressed in jeans, boots and T-shirts, women in pink- or lime-colored polyester shorts, plastic sandals or sneakers and halter-tops. They probably spend the entire day here for $5.99. And why not? The food is plentiful, the music is piped in and the bathrooms have enough seats for everyone.

All you can eat—a concept unheard of back in the old country and probably anywhere else in the world. That's because America produces too much food and has no idea what to do with its excess except for ramming it down our throats. Not that we shouldn't enjoy it. It may very well be our patriotic duty.

That's what I tell Albert and he agrees.

Bits of the food that the customers' throats have missed are trampled into the carpet: macaroni-and-cheese, deep-fried chicken, bacon, hamburgers, potato salad, apple pie. The tables are piled up with half-eaten plates and clean bones. Loud chomping and burping and e-coli fill the air. Kids run underfoot with trays, leaving trails of crumbs like Hansel and Gretel.

The atmosphere should remind me of a pigsty but I've never been to one. I stretch my imagination wider than a party balloon. A pigsty is one of those things that you should recognize even if you have never seen one. It's proverbial. It's literal. It's mainstream. I still fail. Some writer I am.

Albert and I like a hint of danger. Not too much. Not too little. Just right. Danger tickles us. That's what he says. Danger to the soul is like oxygen to the body. That's what I say.

"How's the kids?" I ask Albert. I'm watching a boy carrying a piece of an apple pie in each hand. I make a note for myself to get a cherry pie at my next trip to the dessert counter.

Albert gives me a detailed report. His son flew a remote-controlled plane model and broke a neighbor's window. His daughter locked herself out of the house, and they had to call a locksmith. The bottom line is that his kids are fine. I want to tell him about my kids, but he doesn't ask. I tell him anyway. One of my daughters bought a drum to celebrate the Summer Solstice. My other daughter stepped on the cat's tail and the animal scratched her. The bottom line is that they are fine as well. We both have such fine kids. We both are lucky.

"Want to read my story?" I ask. "Only a thousand words."

He wipes off his hands on a napkin. "Sure."

I chew my chicken leg while watching him blue-pencil my manuscript. It's funny, but I've published more stories than he has though he's a native speaker and has a degree in English. I've already told him how funny it is, on more than one occasion, and he has agreed every time. He has never laughed, though.

Of course, I used to write in Russian, since I was ten. I still remember my first poem. Twenty stanzas like this one, and most even worse:

The sea is violent in the green faraway,
The waves play and jump,
The dark water is carrying ships,
Their masts are sad and forlorn.

I even got my early works published. Back in Yoshkar-Ola, there was a regional newspaper, *Mari Pravda* or *Mari Izvestia*, whatever its name was. It had a literary supplement. I would come to the editor's office, and she would read my articles or poems while I waited in the black vinyl-covered chair. Her name was Irina Abramovna, she was a forty-year-old spinster, and she liked almost everything I brought to her. I think she was in love with me, but she never showed it. She probably considered me virtuous and impenetrable, like Fort Knox. My poems and articles would appear in a week or so, and then I would receive my five or ten rubles in cash. On such occasions, I took my friends to a restaurant to celebrate.

"Buy some stamps," Albert says now when he's done. This is his best compliment. I send most of my magazine submissions via e-mail, but he knows that. I've never seen an American editor face-to-face, and when I'm paid, it's always a check. I deposit it in our family bank account.

I take my manuscript back. The amount of blue on it rivals the black type. It also gets smeared with some tomato sauce, so it looks like Mel Gibson's face in Braveheart. I never liked Mel—he's more opinionated than Torquemada—so I keep the pages away from me with an out-stretched hand.

I wish he'd ask, "Too much blue makes you blue?" or something equally witty, but he doesn't. He eats a pastry. Flakes fall back on his plate like a weird snow. It's summer, actually.

"How's your new girlfriend?" I ask. "Patty, right?"

"She's fine. We went to visit my parents."

"So it's serious?"

"Maybe."

"Will you invite me to the wedding?"

"Sure."

I'm not that sure. He rarely invites me to his house or any other place. It is I who does all the inviting in this friendship.

Outside, sparrows dance on the sidewalk, pecking on crumbs. They look happy. What could be better than free buffet?

"A sparrow is *vorobey* in Russian," I tell Albert. "It literally means *someone who kicks the thief*."

I hope he will ask me why it means that, though I don't know the answer. I can come up with one instantly, though. For example, if they see a thief, they peck him. Or they shit on his head.

Instead of asking, he nods. We go to his car. Two women—no, girls—brush past us, laughing. Tall and ephemeral, they are definitely not the buffet types. Albert and I watch them sail away like the dandelion seeds in the wind.

Albert unlocks the car door and lets it stay open to cool off the insides.

"Why don't you ever ask questions, Albert?" I say. I've asked him this before, more than once, and I know what he is going to say. But I have to ask him. That's who I am.

"That's who I am," he says. I don't question his answer. I watch him drive away. A plume of dark smoke comes from his exhaust pipe. His car needs a tune-up, which he can hardly afford.

That night, I dream that I'm underwater, watching dead sparrows floating on the surface. When I wake up, my heart is a captured bird in my chest. My wife takes me to the emergency room. Ours is a small village, so there is not a single person with a gunshot wound around me. Just two gray-faced older men, and a toddler who fell down the stairs. The toddler, on his mother's lap, yodels. His mother's eyes are huge. I've seen eyes like that on an icon of the Virgin Maria in a Moscow museum. I wonder if my face is also gray.

They fix me fast, but I stay overnight for observation. I refuse to surrender my clothes and keep my jeans on. It's not comfortable to sleep in them, but sleep is out of the question anyway. There is a loudspeaker next to my bed, and it shouts every announcement in the hospital. As soon as I doze off, it reminds me that the hospital, just like New York, New York, never sleeps. I wish I had strength to karate-chop it to pieces.

A nurse comes every hour to check on me. Her face is warm with a smile, but her hands are cold. My wife sits in the chair, pretending to sleep. She refuses to go home in spite of my pleas and the nurse's insistence. I say that a 96-hour shift is too much even for a superwoman, and that I'm in good hands, but my wife says that she can't abandon me because we are two parts of the same being. It's beyond love, she says. Love comes and goes, but you can't severe a half of your body.

I'm lucky that there is no one to share the semi-private room with me. Another sufferer next to me, with his own set of relatives, would have broken my heart with sadness. I'm lucky for once. I won the lottery on that.

A plump dietician comes to offer me my choices of entrees. I'm tempted to make a joke, but I swallow it before it emerges. I can't blame her for her extra weight. She is not a physician, so she doesn't need to heal herself. She suggests baked turkey with mixed vegetables and a roll with margarine. I demand French onion soup and lamb chops. I wouldn't know what to do if she agreed. I don't eat our mammal cousins. After much eye rolling and you-couldn't-do-thats, we settle on baked turkey with mixed vegetables and a roll.

After lunch—I spared the turkey—I doze off.

I descend along the side of a tower, jumping from one narrow ledge to another, occasionally holding on to a rope to steady myself. I have the agility of a chimp, a bird even. No matter how small my next ledge is, I don't miss it. I sing.

Halfway down, I doubt myself. I'm not young anymore. What if I miss the next step? The ground is so far below I'll be just a wet splash. As soon as I think that, I miss the next ledge, and save myself from tumbling down only by hanging on to the rope. I manage to swing to a balcony and grab the railings. I have no strength to climb over it. Several people stand on the balcony, watching me.

"Call 911," I cry.

One of them whips out his cell phone. A cop comes a few minutes later and helps me to safety. I wake up in my hospital bed.

My doctor says that my heart medication causes vivid dreams. He says that I'm lucky because some people take illegal drugs to achieve this effect. I know he's lying. Most people, doctors included, want to be writers. I'm just more creative than he is, and he can't stand the competition.

The next day, after returning from the hospital, I call Albert. He's home and answers on the first ring. It has never happened before. That alone alarms me. I don't need alarms in my present condition.

"I was in the hospital," he says. "I had seizures. I guess it was because of a dream I had. I dreamed about dead girls. We should stop watching movies like that. It's not good for our psyches."

"But you are fine now?" I ask. He's truly my twin. I would want to say that my heart melts, but I'm afraid to damage it further with any well-used allegories.

"Yes," he says. "I'm good now. Thanks for asking."

I imagine him nodding vigorously. I want to ask him if he surrendered his jeans to the nurse with cold hands, and if he had a loudspeaker next to his bed, and if his girlfriend slept in the chair next to him, but I hope he'd ask me a question now. I don't want to interrupt that. I hold my breath. I can hold it for as long as it takes a man's consciousness to rise from the bottom of a dream to its surface.

Keep Sawing, Shura

IT'S STILL 2001. I am still fifty-one. From all the colors of the palette, I like the gold and the red the most, especially when they are combined. Nothing pleases my aesthetics more than a drop of blood on a golden ring.

One busy day, my uncle in my former homeland of Moldova sends me pig-iron utensils. Two large pots and a frying pan packaged in two big cardboard boxes. They probably weigh a ton but I carry them from the post office to the car and from the car to my house. I curse in two languages when no one can hear me.

Moldova used to be a crown jewel in the Soviet Union's proletarian cap. It was a place with a relatively mild climate, great music, cheap wine and plentiful fruits. Now, it's probably the poorest country in Europe. In Moldova, they have heat, water and electricity just a few hours a day. In the winter, ice covers the sidewalks and no one removes it. We sent my uncle slip-on cleats to attach over his shoes. He's in his seventies and fragile like an icicle. He mustn't fall.

In Moldova, bandits break into people's apartments and rob them of their money and possessions. If you are a bit richer than the average, you are in trouble. It only pays off to be very rich but not everyone has enough money for that.

Now, the uncle sends us utensils. It's a puzzle. We don't need puzzles. We are Americans now. We are too busy for headaches.

When my uncle let us know about them in the mail, a month ago, I told my wife, "They are made out of gold."

"Gold?" she said while examining the letter again, perhaps searching for some secret code.

"Yes, gold. Like the metal in this Chinese proverb: 'An inch of time cannot be bought with an inch of gold.'"

"A Chinese proverb? Are you wasting my time with another one of your sick jokes?"

"It's not a joke. I really think it's gold. Unless it's platinum. Painted to resemble pig iron. Remember Ilf and Petrov's *The Golden Calf?*"

Of course, she remembered *The Golden Calf.* In that Russian novel, two characters thought that the dumbbells of a rich man were made out of gold and painted to resemble iron. They stole them and cut them. One character kept telling the other, "Keep sawing, Shura, keep sawing!"

It was iron through and through, after all, so Shura sawed for nothing. I always pitied him.

"Why would he send us utensils made of gold?" my wife said. "He always seemed a sane man."

"Because he wants to transfer his money out of the country. You know how the banking system works in Moldova. They steal everything. He wants us to have the money."

"Even so, where would he get gold in the first place?"

It's a good question. It was illegal to own any substantial quantities of precious metals in the old Soviet Union besides a few personal jewelry items or perhaps a dozen silver spoons. I don't know the current Moldovian laws, but even if gold were legal to own now, where would a piss-poor old man get it?

"Maybe he had the gold since the Romanian times?" I said. "It was legal to own gold in Romania before World War II. Or maybe he received a large inheritance."

My wife shrugged. "You're making things up. Even if he had gold, how would he melt it to make utensils? It's not even literature. It's either science fiction or syrupy romance."

Now, I bring the boxes to the basement. My wife is not home, so there is no need to defend myself against her. Mura follows. She probably hopes for handouts though she's in need of a diet but I hope she wants to keep me company. Hope is cheap.

I unpack the boxes and the cat and I examine the utensils together. They look brand-new. What would I do with the gold? Strike coins with my portrait? Sell it to a jeweler? Hide it in the basement for the rainy day?

The cat finishes sniffing the utensils, and settles nearby, her paws tucked in neatly under her chest. Her eyes suck in all light so I have to watch out so I won't trip over her. Despite her age, she has great eye-to-neck coordination.

I take a file and begin to scratch. The paint comes off easily but the underlying metal resists me. The cat gets up and bangs her head against my knee. The sharp tool catches my finger and a drop of blood falls on the blackness of the pig iron. I pause to admire it. Red against black. It's the second most beautiful thing in the world. But I'm an American now. I have to go on. I shoo away the cat, take the file, and resume my work. The cat hisses. She's also an American but born and raised. She also has to go on.

When I am done, I stare at the filings. They are pure, uncontaminated Russian iron.

"I guess the coins with my portrait are out of the question now," I say to my cat. Her eyes are full of wisdom as if she's a Himalayan guru.

"You have to make it on your own, Shura," they say. I have no choice but to agree.

Down Came the Rain

It's still 2001. I am still fifty-one. The driver's seat with a hole in the shape of Massachusetts slopes the wrong way, and my 205-pound body keeps sliding toward the door with the broken lock. This is the third U-Schlep I've tried. The first one leaked oil and I couldn't shift the second one's transmission into reverse. This truck has bald tires, but the forecast doesn't call for rain. I took it because it's getting late, and I have six hours of driving ahead of me.

From the boom box, *Swan Lake* fails to mask the grunts of the rapidly aging truck, the automotive equivalent of an overweight arthritic in his fifties who forgot to take his daily Aleve. My daughter Mila's furniture rattles in the back. A spider the size of a penny is weaving its web at the edge of the windshield. I shift my bottom back, adjust my bow tie over a T-shirt that says "Engineers do it with precision," and sigh a well-rehearsed sigh.

Mila drives my brand new Toyota Avalon in front of the U-Schlep, her speakers undoubtedly blasting away while she's screaming along, her face locked in concentration. Occasionally she zooms ahead, forgetting about her dad, and I have to shout for her attention through a walkie-talkie.

How I miss the time when she and Rachel sat in the back seat and poked each other in the eye. If someone would have told me back then that in ten years I would consider the backseat fighting, the potty stop requests, and the occasional throwing up the age of innocence, I would've laughed. Yeah, right. I would have said, hah-hah-hah three times. I would have said that the crusades and the Mongol invasion were

the age of innocence. Don't bullshit me, okay? I can tell the age of innocence when I see it. That's what I would have said.

That was then. Now, I see I was wrong. There *was* something appealing in the Mongol invasion. Not innocent, of course, but appealing.
Wild horsemen riding in the wind, bright sabers swooshing in the air,
colorful pendants flowing, blue skies watching, vermillion blood running, yellow skulls grinning. Very picturesque. Even the crusaders look
cool, in their own armored, smelly way, eight hundred years later. Actually, the Mongols were cooler because they encouraged commerce and
cooperation between East and West.

Mongols and crusaders aside, I would give anything except my first
(and second) born to see my two little girls fighting in the backseat once
again.

When Mila was little, we sang together, in English, "The itsy bitsy
spider went up the water spout," and she would cry at "and washed the
spider out." When she grew up, she didn't cry often, but she did when
someone squashed a daddy-long-legs with his fist.

Last week, I found her an apartment to share with two other female
students from Boston University Law School. At $733 her monthly share
is more than I have counted on, that besides tuition.

"The movers are seven hundred bucks more," I told her, in Russian.
"I can't afford them."

"Baloney, Dad. You're rich," she replied in English.

"Watch it, miss! I'm a middle class man. Only lawyers are rich. I
should've stopped supporting you after your bachelor's. Why wouldn't
you take a summer job?"

"And what would you do with your money? Spend it yourself? You
call this parental love? I call this child abuse."

Now, I watch the spider's progress out of the corner of my eye. The sun-
light caught by the emerging web bleeds all the colors of the rainbow.

"You're trespassing, buddy," I say to the spider. "I'll make a citizen's
arrest. You have the right to remain silent. Just look at me! I'm silent."

"Why couldn't she choose a respectable profession?" I continue.
"What's wrong with engineering? She could have spent all day in the
office checking CNN news on the Net and married a future VP. No, she
wants to have a drag race with an ambulance like the rest of the lawyers.
Do you have kids, pal?"

A few thousand trees and two ponds later, I say, "Hey, do you know what I call my daughter now? I call her Sue. Sue! Get it? Not bad for a guy with English as a second language? And you know what she says? 'You can laugh all the way to the bank!'"

A dark cloud covers the sun. It looks like rain, maybe even a thunderstorm.

I see the Avalon zooming again, try to pick up the walkie-talkie, but it falls on the floor. I sigh. The Avalon is getting away.

I step on the worn gas pedal. The U-Schlep jolts, but spurts ahead. We truckers, I think. We rule. We can kick any frigging lawyer's ass!

The truck skids on an oil slick, but I'm able to correct it. The dark cloud grows bigger, eating away the remaining blue portion of the sky like a cancer.

"Kids," I say, wiping sweat from my forehead with the backside of my hand. "You gotta love them."

Fear

It's 2001. I'm fifty-one. My barber tells me that some people spend more than three hours a day on the Internet. He knows everything, and is generous enough to share his wisdom with anyone who faces his mirror. I shake my head and whistle. You don't say.

I spend at least six hours a day on the Net on weekends. I'm a fearless Internet junky. According to my wife, it's time to grow up, but I still spend so much time at my computer that it seems like I know everyone in the world, and the entire world seems to know me. I like everyone, and everyone likes me. At least I deduce that from their desire to communicate. Everyone wants to get in touch with me. They spam me in many languages: English, Russian, Chinese, Japanese, German and French. They spam me in languages I can't recognize let alone understand. Maybe some of these e-mails aren't spam. Maybe they're from an alien race from a distant star that is trying to communicate with earthlings. I will probably never know. Maybe it's for the better. Too much knowledge takes life's surprises away.

Tonight, after work, I got e-mails from a Nigerian colonel, a Russian oil tycoon and an English barrister. All want to give me millions. I admire their selflessness, but the problem is, what would I do with the money? I mean, I know how to spend. I can buy digital cameras, computers, plasma TVs, and PDAs. But that's thousands. To spend millions, you need to climb up to the next level of spending and I hate heights.

I'm not feeling well today. When you stare at the computer screen for too long, you forget to blink, and your eyes get dry. In addition, I'm a bit feverish. It looks like I'm coming down with a virus.

I consider polite replies, but I'm afraid to hurt their feelings. I believe that everybody has feelings, even colonels, tycoons and barristers. So, instead of a polite reply, I send them a cartoon of a man flipping the birdie.

I know it's juvenile, but I can't help myself. I used to play computer games. I considered it a sign that my spirit was still young. The games don't excite me anymore, but modest, innocent pranks like this birdie do. Pranks hint of danger. What if they find out who I am and hack into my computer?

So I send the birdie to the barrister and wait. He may be just a plain phisher and then I'm safe. More or less safe, because there is no absolute safety in this world until you're dead. If he's someone more dangerous, let the games begin and the strongest one win.

I go to the window and peer at the real world outside. Squirrels run up and down the fir trees as if Windows XP had never been invented. A robin pecks at something in the bushes as birds did before the invention of the LCD. The maples wave to me as if I don't have a dual-core processor inside my computer.

I don't reply. We Internet junkies don't mix with nature. We have our own code of honor. I return to the chair, and the mouse grabs my right hand tight as if it wants to grow into my skin. The barrister doesn't respond. He's obviously a wussy, afraid of Americans.

The next morning, François, from the office next to mine, knocks at my wall and shouts, "They bombed the World Trade Center!"

We run to the cafeteria and watch the TV. United Flight 175 from Boston crashes into the South Tower.

"It's the work of the CIA," François says. "Make no mistake."

He was born in Paris, but brought to America as a child. He's tall and blond and dashing when someone buys him a drink, and the office women like him. He has several folders full of conspiracy theory materials in his office. He brags that half of the bookmarks on his Internet Explorer lead to conspiracy websites. His PC's wallpaper is a frame from Abraham Zapruder's film.

He calls me "a world traveler" when others are present. He smirks and winks at the audience when he says that. He says that I can buy a new car every couple of years for the money I spend on travel. He says that I can buy a cottage on a lake or mutual funds or rental property. He asks me how I communicate with the natives. Did I learn how to say, "Baaar, baaar, baaar?" That's how the non-English speakers talk, right? That's why they are called barbarians. Heh-heh-heh.

Now, in the cafeteria, he says that the French hate the Arabs even more than the blacks.

"We should nuke them," John says. "Nuke them and go home."

"Nuke who?" I ask.

"All of them. God will sort them out."

"I knew a Muslim once, and he was OK," Fred, the lab tech says.

John stares him down.

"Well, he always had barbeques on the front lawn," Fred says. "Imagine that? You never know what a man will do until he gets on an airplane."

"They're gonna be sorry," François says. "We will wipe them out. Crush them under our feet. I'm looking forward to it."

"I would enlist if I were younger," John says.

I went to the World Trade Center once. We stood in line behind two German women with hairy armpits. I bought a plastic Lady Liberty crown from a Chinese vendor who was even shorter than my wife. This vendor is probably dead now, and all the crowns are burned to ashes. I wonder what the German women think now? That we deserved it? That you can't hide from hatred even in the tallest building in the world? That they are next?

When I return to the cafeteria two hours later, François is still there by the TV, sitting with his back to me.

"It's the work of the CIA and Mossad," he says to the nodding audience. "The French hate the Jews even more than the Arabs."

I used to tell him that in the old Soviet Union, the French were the ultimate Westerners. I never said anything about frog legs, garlic, impotence, or a tendency for quick surrender.

I return to my office. Fasting is good for the body and soul. It kills fear.

Twelve Steps Down

It's 2002. I am fifty-two. Saskia van Rijn lies across the entrance, guarding her domicile, and doesn't bother to move. She was never thin, but she's bloated to twenty pounds in the last few months. My wife says it's mental—a switch in Saskia's brain doesn't function to tell her shes had enough food already.

I carry a cardboard box in both hands—my soldier's pack—but instead of ammunition and food ration, it holds my coffee cup, books, and pictures. The news I received earlier this morning clings to my shoulders like arthritis, impossible to shake off.

I step over Saskia, nearly losing my balance. Good thing they left me health insurance for a while—transitional, they call it, and the government calls it Cobra, both names threatening and suspicious when you are fifty-three and the economy is shaky.

Twelve steps below, it's chilly and it smells of cat's litter. The fluorescent light flickers, but soon I will have time to fix it. I drop the box on the carpet, next to a fresh stain—oh, Saskia, sweet Saskia! A framed award for my tenth patent and a textbook, *Advancements in Microelectronics*, with my name on the cover, spill from the overturned box. They will be safe for now; it's damp here in the summer, but now the air is dry.

I wipe the dust from a plastic chair with a rug Saskia sleeps on, rub my hands together to get rid of her black, white and brown hair, and sit down. I stare at my fingernails. They are too long, and the ring finger is discolored from a chemical burn. I slump against the back of the chair and close my eyes. The world above me continues its rotation, but I sit still. If I die here, will I dry up and turn into a mummy?

In the back of my mind, I realize that the process of mummification requires outside help, and that Saskia's paws are not suited for such fine work, but I choose to disregard this fact.

Will anybody find me? My wife never comes down; she's afraid to descend below the surface of the earth before her time comes. The kids are off at college. Will anybody care that I'm missing? I'm certain that the traces of my existence are slowly disappearing from the face of the earth. The phone in my former office is being disconnected, my e-mail ID is being erased, my name is being removed from the company's roster. Yes, I will be a mummy; I'll haunt my former boss. I practice a mummy's voice, "I shall return. Prepare to die."

I feel like a dying pharaoh. One day you are the head honcho of the known world, and the next you are draped in linen, they suck your brain out through a straw, and you are destined to curse the tourists of the future.

My boss has no idea what being fifty means. He is thirty-something; he still thinks that he's irreplaceable, that he'll live forever and can find any job he wants.

He told me that it's nothing personal. Just a resource action. They come up with smooth-sounding terms all the time. Restructuring. Downsizing. Buyout. He offered me good references if I needed one. I considered saying something witty to transfer some pain back to him. Like, "They will downsize you next." Or, "Someone will go postal on you and restructure your face." But I only refused to shake his hand.

Now, something soft bumps against my shin. My heart skips. I hope it's a rat, even a giant rat, and nothing worse. I open my eyes. It's Saskia. I swallow. My hands shake.

She puts her paws on my knee and screeches in the voice of an unemployed urban banshee. Hunger glows like a thousand candles inside her eyes. How dare she interrupt such a grave moment for something as prosaic as food? Yet her hunger is contagious. My stomach begins to churn. I get up. She runs upstairs in front of me, kicking with her arthritic paws in her elegant white socks. Left-side limbs, right-side limbs, left-side limbs, right-side limbs, moving like pistons of an indestructible machine. Only cats, giraffes and camels run this way. When she reaches the landing, she turns and glares at me.

I sigh. Will I miss the windowless office, the tired air conditioner, the tasteless cafeteria food and the stale jokes? I grab the rail with my right hand. Gravity sucks out my resolve like a hungry maw. The first step is the hardest. The next one will be easier. I sincerely hope so.

A Report from the

Job Search Front Lines

It's 2003. I am fifty-three. Since I lost my job, I've become even more philosophical than usual, which is of course hard to do when you already are a home-grown Spinoza to begin with. It may be that every unhappy family is unhappy in its own way, but high tech and I were once as happy as two cooing lovers. We loved each other, and our union seemed to grow stronger with every promotion and raise. We still had to part. Unlike in Tolstoy's time, divorce is quick now. No need to jump under the train. It's still painful, though painkillers are more readily available today.

I drive my Avalon past clusters of trailer homes equipped with American flags, Bush-Cheney signs and rusty cars on cinder blocks, all set among the vast parcels of nothingness prowled by squirrels, black bears, skunks, deer and hunters.

New York City people may not know this, but we in Hickland Upstate entered the high-tech era back in the twentieth century. People in other countries may not know that Upstate New York even exists.

I park my Avalon between an aging Beamer and a Jeep with an anti-deer rail welded to the front bumper, and schlep through the puddles, though schlep is a downstate term. I wear business casual—tan pants and an opened collar shirt under a gray jacket—a suburban professional on a job hunt. By the time I get inside, my pant cuffs have turned black from the water. That's OK. The Human Resources people are trained to look at your eyes.

Once in the building, I join one of the many lines. People stand quietly against the ropes. I see a few guys I used to know and I nod to them. They nod to me. No reason to talk. No reason to get out of line. No reason to cross the ropes. We know the rules.

Then I see the manager who laid me off in one of the lines just like the rest of us. Not Fred Wilkinson, who has long since retired and lives in a cottage on a lake that floods him out every other year. The manager who laid me off is overdressed in a suit and tie and shiny wedding shoes. It has been over a year. Over a year of part-time hell. It wasn't his fault. He was doing his job. That's what he said. I said I believed him. We shake hands this time. Just to see him here makes my spirits rise.

"Are you looking for a job?" the manager says now. He probably thinks he is funny. He is growing a bald spot and a potbelly. He's very successful at that.

"No, I'm a correspondent embedded with the 326th job-seeking battalion," I say. I think I'm funny.

"You're still funny, aren't you?" he says. I can only guess what he thinks.

"I'm only focused on finding a job," I say. "You could say I have tunnel vision. Anyway, want my resume?"

He smiles and nods past me. I turn and see a blinding light. Am I dead? Is this the light at the end of the tunnel? Are the moving shadows behind the light angels? On second glance, it's a TV guy and his cameraman.

The next day, a neighbor says, "I saw you on TV. You looked great. But why didn't you wear a tie? Isn't that a must on an interview?"

What does he know? He has a job. Jobs make people blind, fat and dumb. I say, "I'm still learning the ropes."

At least I kept the cameraman employed. Not everyone in my position can claim that and still collect unemployment benefits. Anna Karenina certainly didn't have that much going for her.

A Patriotic Angel

It's still 2003. I am still fifty-three. The angel stands on a shelf in the supermarket aisle reserved for the holiday decorations. She's not tall; maybe five inches maximum. She wears a regulation angel's gown and a red, white and blue scarf about her shoulders in the manner of a priest or a reform Rabbi. She holds a tiny harp, but she doesn't play it.

"What will you play for me?" I ask, bending down to her. "The Star Spangled Banner? Silent Night? A Hanukkah song?" My left hip hurts, but I want to make sure she hears me well.

"Are you working here?" I continue. "Or you came to buy some groceries? Stupid question. Of course, you are working here. As an angel."

I touch the strings of her harp with my finger. They sigh.

"I've never seen your kind before," I press on. "Only everyday, down-to-earth angels . . . What makes you what you are? Do you fly with our pilots to protect them in a battle? Or maybe you advise our government officials and American company CEOs?"

Her plastic fingers move. She plays a few notes from "America the Beautiful." My hip can't stand it any longer. I sit on the floor. Now, our faces are on the same level.

"I'm an immigrant, but now I'm an American patriot. I vote. I pay taxes. I put up the American flag for July 4. We are alike, you and I. We could be friends. Will you ask me questions? I like questions. They give me a chance to answer."

A woman pushes a cart by me. She meets my eyes and purses her lips. I turn to the angel again. "If I take you home, I would have to leave the grapes and the steak here. It's either or. You might be bored at my place; my daughters are already in college and my wife is always at work."

Her eyes say, "Why should I care?" Or, perhaps, "Sure, Daddy."

Outside, the first snowflakes of the night land on my baseball cap. I will listen to five patriotic songs tonight, playing in the sequence of my choice, in the company of an angel, while drinking milk and eating bread. What more can a man possibly want?

The Battlefield of Justice

and the American Way

IT'S 2004. I am fifty-four. No one wants to hire me. I'm getting too hairless and hoary. This is the first job I've got in a while, and I had better do it well. Or at least, to take a cue from our politicians, create an impression of a job well done.

I slouch forward so that the judge won't see what I'm doing. My client sits next to me, listening very carefully to what the judge is saying, but probably understanding very little. If he knew English, I wouldn't be here. The client wears a blue denim shirt, suede boots and jeans; a lumberjack, a redneck by the looks of him. Rednecks are like roaches except you can't squish them. That's not what I think. That's what my New York City friends say.

I will be paid $62.50 for my services. With two hundred dollars I stashed away from similar battles, I'll be able to buy a Pentium 4 chip and upgrade my aging computer. Unless I make the same costly mistake that I did last time. But I won't. A general who never learns from his mistakes is not worth his stripes. Or stars. Or chips. Or whatever they wear on their sleeves. I have to look it up online. After all, English is not my first language either. Twenty-four years of living in America, and my best efforts still can't erase this fact. I can twist the language into something deliciously weird more easily than your average native, but I can't feel it the way even a child could.

It's ninety degrees outside, and the air conditioner is sluggish. I don't sweat anymore; I'm too thin now.

A short, bowlegged and muscular Asian man is describing the scene of the accident to the judge. He stumbles through the intricacy of the English language, but marches ahead boldly, a Tamerlane on horseback. The assistant DA, a Caucasian woman in size 3X clothes, entrenched behind her table, shoots questions at him, each one a sharp arrow, a biting javelin.

"What is *moofin fiolation*?" she asks him. "Ah, you mean 'moving violation'?"

She wipes sweat from her forehead with a handkerchief that can't absorb any more fluids.

I sigh and return to the *PC Magazine* on my lap.

"Next case," the bailiff calls. "People of New York against Vladimir Titov." He stresses a wrong syllable—"vlad" instead of "dim" as if my client Vladimir is some kind of a smart Dracula.

Vladimir and I approach the bench. I would like to say that all eyes are on us, but I would be lying. Even the eyes that are on us are glazed over.

The judge asks Vladimir to state his name and before I interpret the question, Vladimir answers in English. The judge frowns.

"If you understand English why did you force us to spend money on the interpreter?" she says, pointing an accusative finger at Vladimir and a dismissive one at me. I freeze. "Maybe you thought he'd give you legal advice? He can't. He's not a lawyer."

This is a critical juncture. If the sword of justice cuts Vladimir in half, will I still be paid? Will the judge dismiss me? I wish I could put Russian words into my client's mouth. Buddy, hey buddy? Say, I know basic English, but the court procedures are too complicated for me.

Come on, say it, buddy! You stinking foreign roach. You come here to take jobs from the Americans. I should do this society a favor and squish you under my foot.

I turn to the assistant DA who tries to mop her neck.

It's saturated already. You little piggy, I think in Russian.

Vladimir opens his mouth and releases the smell of onion. I hate onions, though I like garlic. The three of us watch Vladimir draw a breath.

"Hell, yes, I know English, but you guys are talking gibberish in here," he says in Russian.

I translate that with the rapid burst of a Gatling gun—I know basic English, but the court procedures are too complicated for me—and the judge nods. The assistant DA takes a paper napkin from the table and wipes her neck.

"Please don't fine me," Vladimir says in Russian. "I'm broke."

I translate, feeling a drop of sweat coming down my neck. Why should I care? As the Russians say, *les rubyat, schepki letayat*—when you cut wood, the chips fly. The Pentium is practically in my hands. That's all that counts.

"You should have thought about that when you didn't stop at the red light," the judge said.

Vladimir stoops and covers his face with his hands as if posing for the courthouse-bound painting called *Penitence in the House of Law*.

Ten minutes later, Vladimir and I are outside.

"One hundred twenty dollars and three points on my license," Vladimir says, in Russian. "Will they throw me in jail if I don't pay?"

"They might take your license away," I say carefully. As the judge said, I'm not supposed to give legal advice. "I know it's tough. I'm a recent immigrant myself."

"What will I tell my wife?"

Another drop of sweat travels down my spine. My brother knows how to handle situations like this. Should I call him on my cell?

You know, Volodya, there is this guy who is poor, and he needs help, and I don't have much money myself, and what I do have, I need for an important project, so what should I do? Naah. It would sound stupid because it is.

"They are going to evict us," Vladimir says. "What will I do?"

I pull two crisp twenty-dollar bills from my wallet and hand them to Vladimir. What the hell am I doing? I think in English. Didn't I promise myself to quit making these kinds of mistakes again?

Vladimir shakes my hand. His palm is wet. Thank yous drop from his lips like victory leaflets. He limps away.

I brush off the invisible chips from the sleeve of my jacket. I wonder if I could overdrive my Pentium by using a bigger fan. What are the synonyms for "limp"? Gait? I have to look it up online. The Net has all the answers. And as for me, all I have to do is pretend it's true.

Vae Victis

IT'S STILL 2004. I am still fifty-four. I'm shopping for groceries, and now am pushing my cart toward the cashiers. I'm the default shopper in my family. My wife is working, as always. Someone has to work to support the rest of us. I'm alone with a cat that only either sleeps or poops on the carpet.

According to her nametag, the cashier's name is Wanda. The zits on her face form the letter "W," or, to put it a different way, are the shape of the beautiful constellation Cassiopeia.

"$15.66," Wanda says, her gaze adrift like a child lost in the forest.

"1566?" I say. "That's the year Nostradamus died."

She doesn't smile, waiting for me to share the contents of my wallet with her. Perhaps she doesn't understand my accent. Perhaps she doesn't care. Perhaps she thinks that Nostradamus was a con artist whose prophecies were overblown by impressionable youths and conspiracy theorists. Life has treated Wanda like a patiently abusive husband, adding wrinkles, skin blemishes and crow's feet instead of broken bones and black eyes.

"I'm going to the Ukraine," I say. "I'll be an international observer for the election. It's the run-off election for the president."

I know it sounds too grand. I have registered with the Ukrainian Canadian Congress to monitor the elections though I'm neither Ukrainian nor Canadian. I'm no longer sure what I am. An aging man with no job? That's as good a description as any.

"They will pay for my meals and lodging, but I have to buy my own ticket and pay the visa fee," I say. "They might reimburse me later. They better. My unemployment benefits have run out."

"We don't take Visa here. Only Discover."

I have seen such vacant eyes on a nineteenth-century postmortem photograph: a young woman holding a dead baby swathed in white, wilting roses clinging to its chest.

"Nostradamus never predicted which of the Victors would be the victor," I say. "Victor Yushchenko or Victor Yanukovych. Do you know that the word 'victor' comes from the Latin word *victis*, past participle of *vincere*, to conquer? *Victis* may also mean 'conquered.' I'm not so good in Latin."

"Sir, you are, like, holding up the line."

I glance over my shoulder. No one is behind me. I rummage through my wallet and produce a Discover card.

"I was born in Russia but I've lived here for twenty-four years. Does that mean I am an American now?"

She leans over and snatches the card from my hand.

"America supports Yushchenko. Some of the friends I went to school with in Moscow support Yanukovych. They say Yushchenko is a nationalist. They say he is against Russian-speakers. My friend's wife spoke Ukrainian at home but my friend spoke Russian. He called her *hohlushka* and she called him *katsap*. It's like calling someone 'nigger' or 'kike'."

"Sign at the X."

I scribble my name on the screen. My signature doesn't look like anything I have ever produced on paper. Do I have to sign my name in Ukrainian once I arrive in Kiev? I remember vaguely that some Cyrillic letters were mutilated by the Ukrainians. Or was it the Russians who mutilated them, as my friend's wife would claim in the heat of an argument?

I'll stay for a few days with my classmate Petr, who has to Ukranianize his name to Petro. I can't stay longer; Petro's family of five lives in a one-bedroom apartment. A sad state of affairs for an engineer with twenty-five years of experience. On the other hand, Petro still has a job and his family is with him.

I look forward to living in a dorm again, after my stay with Petro. What will they have on the wall instead of a Lenin? Gogol's Taras Bulba with a sword in his hand, on a black stallion with a set of iron testicles the size of cannon balls, riding majestically on its hind legs? An icon of Isus Hristos? A centerfold from the Russian edition of *Playboy*?

And the girls. Are they still as beautiful as they were thirty years ago? That's a question of pure aesthetics, of course. I'm happily married.

How about food? They should certainly have better food now. Some *varenyky, holubtsi, galushkis*. Yummy. No lines, too.

How about the KGB or whatever they call them now? Will they harass the observers as they used to do? Do they still have the old-style KGB colonel, a man in the windowless interrogation room lit by a bare five-hundred-watt lamp suspended from the ceiling on a snake of a cord, a mandatory Lenin (or was it Felix Dzerzhinsky?) hanging on the wall behind him, matching the colonel's stare? I doubt it. It's the twenty-first century now. There is probably an identical room but with more high-tech equipment. There is probably an identical-looking colonel, cloned in a KGB underground lab, but with a blue-and-yellow shoulder patch on his sleeve instead of the sickle and hammer.

And I look forward to seeing my other classmate Oleg, a New Russian, er, a New Ukrainian, if he can find time to pick me up in his bullet-proof Mercedes 500 and take me to his tastelessly decorated million-dollar office, while showing off his five-thousand-dollar tie, three-thousand-dollar boots and priceless suit.

"Sir! I'm calling security," Wanda says.

Hatred rises to the surface of her eyes, breaking through the ice of her vacant gaze. I glance over my shoulder. Another cashier stands close by, solid like an SS Sturmbannführer, his muscular hands folded on his chest.

"I'm sorry I talk too much," I say. "I have no one to talk to. I'm sorry. I hoped my brother would come here, but the government never gave him the entry visa. So he went to Israel instead. He's my only brother. We are like two peas in a pod. Two sad, wilted peas."

I pick up my bag and inch toward the exit, feeling the woman's stare on my back like the barrel of a gun against my spine.

She wouldn't dare shoot me in public, I think. I'm a diplomat. I represent American democracy in the third world. I will teach the aborigines how to build a better life. I will lead the way. I will persevere. I will look down the barrel of history like Nostradamus.

I straighten up. I suck in my stomach. I raise my chin. I'm ready to face the colonel's clone. I will prevail against him. Vae victis and woe to the vanquished. Nostradamus would be proud of me.

On the other hand, I still have a cat at home. Just like a schizophrenic can never be alone, so can't be a man with a cat.

Basileus

It's 2005. I am fifty-five. On the one hand, I hate him. On the other hand, I love him. But maybe I've got things mixed up. Maybe I love him on the one hand and hate on the other. I'm so pressured I can't tell one limb from another.

He runs right in front of me, and I'm afraid I'll trip over him. He leaves clumps of hair on every surface. Sometimes he locks his paws over my slippers and bites the soles. He jumps on the table, scratches furniture and claws the toilet paper.

When my old cat of ten years died—she was such a chubby sweetheart—my daughter Rachel and I adopted this new cat from the Humane Society. We paid the $85 adoption fee, and filled out paperwork as extensive as if he were a human boy and not a one-year-old neutered Tom. We liked him because he seemed quieter than the others, and he had a round head like our old cat, instead of the ugly, angular head of a regular feline. Now Rachel is back on campus, my wife is always at work, and I'm stuck with him.

The old cat died while in the care of a family friend, who is no longer a friend. We went away to Hawaii to entertain our Russian guests. When we came home, the old cat was dead. We had the option to bury her or have her cremated. If we chose the latter, they would have given us a box with ashes to put on the mantel. We arranged a group cremation instead—let her soul mingle with the souls of other cats. Our mantel is too dusty anyway.

The new cat, though he weighs only half of what my old one used to weigh, stinks. My wife and Rachel say it's because he's male. My wife calls him Basileus, which means "king" in Greek. It's a common Russian name for male cats. Don't ask.

Abraham from the synagogue says that religious Jews shouldn't have pets. It's not a hard-and-fast rule, but a recommendation.

"Why?" I ask.

All my conversations with him inevitably involve this three-letter word.

"Because Nazis used dogs against the Jews in the camps," he says.

He always gets me when I least expect it. I probably resemble a fish now, opening and closing my mouth with no sound coming out. He watches me with the harsh satisfaction of a Galilean fisherman.

"I have a cat," I finally say. "Unlike you, I lost family in the Holocaust, but did Nazis use cats against the Jews? And also, if Nazis had sex, does it mean that we can't have it?"

Abraham's face turns red and he says "heretic" under his breath. Our conversations always end with this seven-letter word. Start with a three and end with a seven. That's progress.

When I come home, I rename the cat from Basileus to *Hitlerjugend*, which means Hitler-Youth, HJ for short.

HJ, don't scratch the furniture! HJ, don't claw the toilet paper! HJ, you Nazi bastard, go to hell!

I go to the spare bedroom, which is my office, and close the door behind me. He waits outside, ready to pounce. His patience has no limits, and he's skilled with his paws. I feel besieged. I know that eventually he will build a trebuchet and take the door down.

On the other hand, when HJ rubs his head against my slippers instead of biting them, my heart liquefies. I have been surrounded by females in my family, so HJ and I, we should bond.

I tap my knee, which is his cue. He jumps on my lap, and walks back and forth, his bushy tail in my nose, until he settles down to sleep. He looks so innocent. He would never throw a stone through the plated glass window of a Jewish store.

I also snooze, and I walk on a white cloud, holding my late cat, all twenty pounds of her, close to my chest.

"How's life?" she purrs.

"Well, HJ jumps on the table all the time. You never did that."

"I did. When I was younger."

I drop her, and she bounces on the cloud below. "You did?"

"Did what?"

The last question wasn't a purr. I open my eyes. It's my wife. She takes HJ—Basileus, and walks away. I can't tell her about my dream. It's a bad omen to talk to the dead, even dead cats.

Basileus purrs on my wife's chest. They bonded so nicely. I'm envious. Maybe I should get a German shepherd to bond to. On the other hand, Basileus will eventually gain another ten pounds. It might take him a while, though.

Thanksgiving

IT'S 2006. I am fifty-six. It rains hard on the way to Massachusetts. I drive at the speed limit, afraid of hydroplaning. Normally, I'm brave, going seventy in the sixty-five-mile zone.

My brother Volodya sits next to me. It took him twenty-six years, but he finally made it here, if only as a tourist. His wife and he are not bitter.

He says, "I wish it'd rain like this in Israel. We have very little rain there."

The first time he said that was when we crossed the Broome county border. Then he repeated this observation when we passed Oneonta. Now we are entering Albany city limits. I can hardly see the road. The gods of rain are working overtime today.

"People fight for the land and they fight for water in Israel," my brother says. "No one fights for water here. Aren't you guys lucky?"

Sylvia sits in the back between Lyuba and Rachel. My niece stayed behind in Israel. She just got married to a Sabra, an Israeli native, and they are busy weaving a family nest in a suburb of Tel Aviv. It takes a lot of feathers and twigs for this time-consuming job.

"I'd never leave Israel," Sylvia says. "I'm a patriot."

We speak in Russian, of course. That's how American patriots communicate with Israeli patriots.

"How far is that place from Boston, again?" Sylvia asks. "Right, Vooster, thank you. How far?"

"A gazillion tons of water," I say. "West of Eden."

After dinner tonight, I will corner everyone one by one, and ask what they think about me. I'll tell them to be honest and spare nothing. Every writer is nosey, and I'm a writer.

When we arrive at my wife's sister's house, Stella and her husband Piotr greet us by the door. His hair is a dignified gray. You might take him for a diplomat or a wealthy socialite if you squint and manage to concentrate on his hair.

"Still shedding your hair, Tommy?" he says to me, grinning. He calls me Tommy because my wife calls me Tomcat. It's a hoary joke, but he grins every time.

"When are you due?" I ask, pointing to his belly, which hangs there like a bag of yesterday's donuts. We don't shake hands.

"Stop it, stop it, boys," Stella says. She hugs everyone. She is four years older than my wife, but looks like her slightly more tired twin.

"Welcome to America," she tells Volodya. "How long has it been since we saw each other last?"

"Twenty-six years," he says. "You haven't changed much."

Boy, he's still smooth.

Half an hour later, I sit on the living room couch of my in-laws' condo, listening to the women's chat, a glass of non-alcoholic wine in my hand. Stella has already given the Israeli guests the tour of the condo. Volodya and Piotr smoke on the porch. I can see them through the window, laughing and slapping each other on the shoulders.

"Piotr smokes almost a pack a day," my sister-in-law says.

"Mine smokes three cigarettes a day at most," Sylvia says. "I almost never smoke. Tobacco makes your teeth yellow."

Mila and my two nephews arrive from Boston, in three separate cars. What a waste of resources. They all are spaced exactly four years apart: Rachel, the youngest; my younger nephew; Mila; and my senior nephew. They all are professionals: a lawyer and two engineers and a biology major. We are proud of them.

Today is Mila's birthday and tomorrow is her sister's. She was a gift for Mila on her eighth birthday.

"Happy Thanksgiving," the next generation shouts from the door in imperfect unison, in English, naturally.

We sit at the long table in the kitchen, under antique paintings of food. We eat turkey with cranberry sauce, stuffing on the side (too many calories), lamb shish kebabs and green salad. I eat chicken kebab.

Piotr made it just for me because I don't eat red meat. He tells that to everyone. He makes toasts to Thanksgiving, my daughter's birthday, the foreign guests' arrival, friendship and health. We bang our glasses obediently.

"Great lamb kebabs," Piotr says. "You can't have it, Tommy."

For dessert they serve fruits, nuts, pastries, Jell-O and chocolate candies. Piotr arranges the fruit plate in the shape of a castle. He's a master decorator.

We chat about work, Middle East politics and children. Piotr tells jokes. I snap everyone's pictures, except for Piotr and the nephews because they object. I wanted to question them, "Why do you object to immortality?" but continue snapping instead.

"How's life?" I ask the nephews. "When are you going to marry?"

They inform me that life is good, that they have no nuptial plans yet, and inquire about the state of my health and my literary successes. I tell them that I am fine, and that my writing life couldn't get any better.

When they had just arrived in America, fifteen years ago, the three of them stayed in our house for six months, until their mother found a job and arranged for Piotr's arrival from Moldova. They all moved to Massachusetts when she found a job there.

My brother tells us how Israeli engineers work. We compare notes. It turns out that it's all about the same. The management squeezes the workers, and what can you do? You need to feed your family or buy a luxury car or travel to Florida.

I corner Stella, each of the nephews, my daughters, Sylvia and my brother.

"What do I think of you?" each of them says thoughtfully as if they never imagined that I could pop such a question. Don't they know writers are nosey? "You're fine. You're OK."

My kids add to this that they love me, but only if I can be a little less stern. Sylvia adds that I'm still handsome and asks how much this condo costs. Stella adds that she's grateful to me that I drove my family here since my wife and Rachel don't like to drive. Volodya adds that we should meet more often, and that it's too bad that our parents are in frail health and couldn't come here as well. Each nephew adds two new jokes.

The boys depart late in the evening. They rent their own places a short distance away. My older daughter stays. My family sleeps on air mattresses on the living room floor. My brother and his wife, the foreign guests, take the spare bedroom.

At night, I can hear Piotr coughing and wheezing. I watch the stars through the skylight until they fade into the rising sun. My old enemy Stalin liked to stay up late. Maybe he was a bit more complicated than your average boogieman in the closet after all. Maybe he also was a torturing and a tortured soul.

In the morning, after breakfast, which is much bigger than I normally have, I corner Piotr.

"What do I think of you?" he says. "You talk too much."

We drive to Boston and tour the downtown. The foreign guests are impressed, though they are disappointed to see my older daughter's tiny rental apartment. That's a Russian apartment, a typical Khrushchev slum, they say. My brother snaps pictures. They buy presents for their daughter and her husband.

Piotr stayed behind. He's seen it all, he says.

When we come back, I happen to sit next to him at dinner. He runs out of jokes, and chews thoughtfully on the turkey's skin. His wife tells him how unhealthy it is. Only fat and cholesterol. My wife chimes in to support her sister. I say, leave the man alone. When Piotr runs out of skin, he tells me that he recently had an irregular heartbeat. I had one, too. We discuss that at length—the symptoms, the treatment, the chances for recurrence, the stupid, overbearing reaction of the family. Piotr shows me and my brother his power tools in the basement and complains about his wife's control over his life. My brother says that all women are control freaks. Piotr tells a joke. My brother tells a joke as well. We all laugh, power males in our prime, surrounded by comfort and loving families.

When we depart, Piotr shakes my hand and advises me to drive safely. So does his wife. I promise. It's my duty to protect my extended family. That's what I live for now. The driving promises to be easy. It's sunny, warm, and the forecast calls for no rain.

When we are approaching home, I see Mr. Simpson's houseguest making a K-turn in my driveway. Mr. Simpson stands on his porch. I wave to him, but he pretends I'm a fly. There are six SUVs parked in his driveway.

Later, my brother smokes on the porch. I stand upwind from him.

"I won't come to your house ever again," he says.

"Why?"

He sends a puff of smoke to the low sky. "Because you don't give me enough attention. Your wife never talks to us. There is nothing to do in your village. And that barking dog. Not enough reasons for you?"

The next morning, I drive Sylvia and him to JFK airport. We listen to Israeli songs on the CD. Sylvia sings along. She has a great voice.

"Keep the CD," Volodya says when we arrive. I sing the American anthem on the way back, though I know only the first four lines by heart.

But I still have Annie, and no one can take that away.

Annie and I add cameras to our computers, so we can see each other. She still talks about the students, and I still tell her jokes. One of these days, the technology will let us touch remotely.

But the problem is, the more I study and learn, the more I'm convinced that I'm not Jacob, and I have to make a choice. Now, in this world, and not after I die. I can't carry this uncertainty for much longer. The weight of it makes me stooped and frail. I set up the dates for the decision several times, but kept postponing it. Tomorrow, when Annie's image appears on my screen, I will tell her what my choice is. There can be only one *bashert* for me. I'm sure that she feels the same, and will drop Barry. He is like a cannon ball that drags her down.

When I turn the computer on, I see Barry next to her. They keep their hands on each other's shoulders the way I picture Annie and I would do one day.

"How've you been, Alex?" Barry shouts with a wide grin. "Haven't seen you for a while! Have you got a joke for us?"

I mutter something and turn the computer off.

A more emotional guy would commit suicide, write a haiku or challenge Barry to a duel. But I'm my father's son and so I'm stoic. As Saint Augustine said, patience is the companion of wisdom. On the other hand, I'm no saint.

Thanks to the wonders of technology, I can see myself in a little window on screen as if in a mirror. The man in front of me, an older guy, who some might even call a gentleman, looks dignified and composed, though his life is ruined. Yet he still has one *bashert* left. I pity him and I envy him.

My mother calls me the following day. "They arrived safely," she reports. "I wish your father and I could come see you. We miss you and the grandkids so."

"I miss you, too," I say.

I wish I could tell her more. Like, for example, everything. I wish I could tell her my life story, which I keep away from her and everyone else. I wish I could tell her bad news and good news. The bad news is that a life can't be declared a success while the person is still alive. The good news is that it can't be declared a failure. I've been a wanderer, carried all over the world like dust by the wind, and I wish I could tell her that every person lugs his made-on-demand paradise and hell with him across the borders, and that customs won't confiscate your burden even if you beg or karate chop them. I wish I could tell her that I'm happy just because I have fingers to type, eyes to see a monitor and the mouth to complain to tech support. According to the Talmud, a man reaches fullness of years at seventy and spiritual strength at eighty. I could tell her that I have a long way to go.

I wish I could welcome her to my story because every narrator needs an intelligent reader. But I'm too selfish to share and too shy for exposure. Instead of spilling everything, I say goodbye and hang up.

Only then, in the safety of my bedroom, watching the phone sitting securely in its cradle, I tell my mother everything. After all, I'm a writer. I can't keep things to myself. According to the ancient Greeks, it's hubris. As Rachel, a biology major, once told me, old trees sprout beautiful flowers before they die. So, like a nomad, like a reindeer driver, I sing about what I saw.

Acknowledgments

I wish I could say that I wrote this book with a pen of iron with the point of a diamond upon the tablet of my heart. Yet this kind of writing is not my style, and these words have already been taken by a writer infinitely better than I.

I wrote this book in its final form on my computer, in the overstuffed comfort of a spare bedroom in my suburban house, but it began to shape in my mind as soon as I discovered what the words "shape" and "mind" are.

It may not be the story of my life as it actually happened, and definitely not as I wish it happened. It's the story of a typical man of my background and generation, whose dreams, nightmares, desires, failures, and accomplishments I still feel inside my skin.

Tragedy makes a rich blood meal for a growing plant. Comedy adds water. This book is a balance of both.

I would like to thank my agent Byrd Leavell, who believed in me and fought for me, breaking many spears in this fight. I am thankful to my Counterpoint editors Maris Kreizman, Trish Hoard, Roxanna Aliaga, and Laura Mazer who worked hard and were helpful beyond the call of duty. They burned the midnight oil for me ($140 a barrel at the time of this writing).

Above all, I would like to thank my family for what they are. Without you, this book wouldn't have happened.